YORK NOTES

Our Day Out

Willy Russell
with Songs by Bob Eaton, Chris Mellor
& Willy Russell

Notes by Chrissie Wright

Longman York Press

YORK PRESS
322 Old Brompton Road, London SW5 9JH

ADDISON WESLEY LONGMAN LIMITED
Edinburgh Gate, Harlow,
Essex CM20 2JE, United Kingdom
Associated companies, branches and representatives throughout the world

First published 1998

ISBN 0–582–36837–5

Designed by Vicki Pacey, Trojan Horse, London
Illustrations by Adam Stower
Phototypeset by Gem Graphics, Trenance, Mawgan Porth, Cornwall
Colour reproduction and film output by Spectrum Colour
Produced by Addison Wesley Longman China Limited, Hong Kong

Contents

PREFACE

York Notes are designed to give you a broader perspective on works of literature studied at GCSE and equivalent levels. We have carried out extensive research into the needs of the modern literature student prior to publishing this new edition. Our research showed that no existing series fully met students' requirements. Rather than present a single authoritative approach, we have provided alternative viewpoints, empowering students to reach their own interpretations of the text. York Notes provide a close examination of the work and include biographical and historical background, summaries, glossaries, analyses of characters, themes, structure and language, cultural connections and literary terms.

If you look at the Contents page you will see the structure for the series. However, there's no need to read from the beginning to the end as you would with a novel, play, poem or short story. Use the Notes in the way that suits you. Our aim is to help you with your understanding of the work, not to dictate how you should learn.

York Notes are written by English teachers and examiners, with an expert knowledge of the subject. They show you how to succeed in coursework and examination assignments, guiding you through the text and offering practical advice. Questions and comments will extend, test and reinforce your knowledge. Attractive colour design and illustrations improve clarity and understanding, making these Notes easy to use and handy for quick reference.

York Notes are ideal for:
- Essay writing
- Exam preparation
- Class discussion

The author of these notes is Chrissie Wright, an ex-head of English and the head teacher of a school in Middlesbrough. She was educated at Durham University and the Open University, and works as a Principal Examiner for GCSE English and English Literature.

The text used in these Notes is the Methuen Young Drama edition (1984, reprinted 1997).

Health Warning: **This study guide will enhance your understanding, but should not replace the reading of the original text and/or study in class.**

PART ONE

INTRODUCTION

HOW TO STUDY A PLAY

You have bought this book because you wanted to study a play on your own. This may supplement classwork.

- Drama is a special 'kind' of writing (the technical term is 'genre') because it needs a performance in the theatre to arrive at a full interpretation of its meaning. When reading a play you have to imagine how it should be performed; the words alone will not be sufficient. Think of gestures and movements.

- Drama is always about conflict of some sort (it may be below the surface). Identify the conflicts in the play and you will be close to identifying the large ideas or themes which bind all the parts together.

- Make careful notes on themes, characters, plot and any sub-plots of the play.

- Playwrights find non-realistic ways of allowing an audience to see into the minds and motives of their characters. The 'soliloquy', in which a character speaks directly to the audience, is one such device. Does the play you are studying have any such passages?

- Which characters do you like or dislike in the play? Why? Do your sympathies change as you see more of these characters?

- Think of the playwright writing the play. Why were these particular arrangements of events, these particular sets of characters and these particular speeches chosen?

Studying on your own requires self-discipline and a carefully thought-out work plan in order to be effective. Good luck.

WILLY RUSSELL'S BACKGROUND

How he came to be a playwright

Willy Russell was born in Whiston, near Liverpool, and left school at fifteen. He took a succession of jobs before he was twenty, when he decided to resume his education. He took GCE 'O' and 'A' levels, intending to become a teacher. At that time, however, he happened to see John McGrath's play, *Unruly Elements*, at the Everyman Theatre, Liverpool, and decided instead to try to become a playwright. He began with a play for the 1972 Edinburgh Festival, *Blind Scouse*, and his first successful play at the Liverpool Everyman Theatre was *John, Paul, George, Ringo and … Bert*, a **musical** (see Literary Terms) about the Beatles and their era. He has also written *Breezeblock Park*, a **comedy** (see Literary Terms), *One for the Road*, *Stags and Hens*, *Educating Rita*, *Blood Brothers*, a **musical**, and *Shirley Valentine*.

Consider how Willy Russell's early end to education might have influenced his views.

During the 1970s he wrote several plays for television, including the original *Our Day Out*, which was broadcast as a BBC Play for Today in 1976. The play was subsequently adapted for the stage, with a musical score added, and first seen at the Everyman Theatre in 1983.

Willy Russell was Writer in Residence at C.F. Mott College, Liverpool, in 1976, and from 1977 to 1979 he was a Fellow in Creative Writing at what was then Manchester Polytechnic. He is a founder and director of Quintet Films. In June 1983 the Open University awarded him an Honorary MA in recognition of his work as a playwright.

Several of Willy Russell's plays have been successfully adapted for film or television. *Educating Rita* was filmed in 1983, starring Michael Caine and Julie Walters, a film for which Russell wrote the screenplay. *Shirley Valentine* was filmed in 1990, and *Stags and Hens*, the **comedy** which takes place in the Ladies and

Gents of a Liverpool night club, was adapted as a made-for-television film, *Dancin' Thru' the Dark*.

Themes in Willy Russell's writing

Willy Russell often writes about education, either formal or otherwise. He has perhaps been influenced by his own late start in education. In *Our Day Out* and *Educating Rita*, he explores the effect that being working class and poor or deprived can have on people's educational chances and how this affects their whole life and the opportunities open to them. A common theme in many of his plays is waste, especially the waste of talent and potential among deprived young people whose futures are shaped by their environment. He often contrasts **characters** (see Literary Terms) who are more privileged with those who are not, and looks at the contrasts between their lives and the opportunities they have. Most of his plays are **comedies** (see Literary Terms) of the sort that has the audiences roaring with laughter, but underlying all of them is a serious theme, and it is rare to come out of a performance of a Willy Russell play or to watch a film adapted from a stage performance without feeling that you have been made to think, as well as having been entertained.

There are frequent contrasts in his plays between privileged and deprived children.

CONTEXT & SETTING

The 'Progress Class' have many problems in their lives.

Our Day Out was first written as a BBC play in the mid 1970s, and reflects social and economic conditions in working-class Liverpool at that time. It is set in an inner-city comprehensive school whose catchment area is deprived and where there are many poor or single-parent families with high unemployment and few opportunities for young people leaving school. The 'Progress Class' whose day out is shown in the play are at the tail end of the queue when it comes to opportunity, even in this area. They are the underachievers, the backward, with low reading ages, poor academic abilities and little chance of passing any examinations, still less of getting a job when they leave school.

As the play was adapted for the stage as a **musical** (see Literary Terms) during the 1980s, the recession had deepened in Liverpool, and opportunities for these youngsters had perhaps receded still further.

Liverpool is famed for its sense of humour, a humour underpinned by gritty **realism** (see Literary Terms), and much of this humour comes across in the play. It tells the story of what happens when Mrs Kay, the Progress Class's liberal teacher, takes her group for a day out to Wales, accompanied by two young teachers and the strict Mr Briggs who is sent along by the head teacher to keep order. The play can be read on more than one level. It is a delightfully comic celebration of the joys and agonies of being a teenager free from school for the day, but, in contrast, it highlights the depressing present and the empty future for the low achievers from inner-city Liverpool, for whom a 'good day out' is about as much as they dare expect. The adult argument is presented throughout the play by the staff, and both contrasts with and complements the fun of the children's story as they collectively get into as much mischief as they can on their day out. The words to the songs reinforce the fun and warmth of the story, but also highlight the sense of bleakness in the prospect they offer of a wasted future for so many children.

The play is both comic and serious and can be read on more than one level.

Our Day Out is often considered by teachers of English and examination boards to be suitable only for less able pupils: a mistake. There is enough serious philosophical material in it to make it worth consideration, enjoyment and performance by all pupils, and mixed-ability groups working in class or on a school production have often gained a great deal from the play, not only in terms of fun but also in the sense that they have been forced by the quality of writing to consider several serious issues and questions about society and education and its purpose.

COMPREHENSIVE SCHOOLS IN THE 1970S – EARLY 1980S

By the mid 1970s most of Britain's schools had become comprehensive, taking in children of all abilities from their local area. In one sense, however, there were still huge differences between schools. Contrast a comprehensive school from an affluent, middle-class suburb – where most parents have professional jobs, and houses are luxurious semis or detached, with garages, large gardens and two or more cars parked outside – with an inner-city school where the houses are crammed into small terraces with no space to play, and most parents do not have jobs, cars or holidays. In financial terms alone there would be a difference: parents from the well-off suburb could afford school trips abroad for their youngsters; fund-raising for extras such as minibuses, music and computers would be successful, and there would be every encouragement for children to work harder when they saw their parents who had passed examinations in successful high-earning jobs. Where parents and older brothers and sisters are unemployed, however, and there is no money for basics like food and rent, let alone extras, even bright children must feel that it is hardly worth working to pass examinations when there may be no jobs for them. Looking at the prospects for the least able children: during the 1960s when there was full employment they would have got jobs in factories or shops, or labouring, where examination passes were not required. By the mid to late 1970s there was an economic recession; most inner-city factories had closed

Consider the difference between a school in the 'leafy suburbs' and one in an inner-city area.

down and many unskilled labouring jobs had simply disappeared. There was no room for the unskilled young person in the labour market.

Schools in different areas, therefore, were very different places, with children in the type of school depicted in *Our Day Out* being harder to motivate, especially the less able. Teachers like Mrs Kay (see Characters and Themes) tried to do their best for the pupils by at least being nice to them, attempting to raise their self-esteem and giving them a treat when possible. Mr Briggs, however, represents a different type of teacher who often fails to understand the enormous social and economic pressures faced by deprived, less able youngsters, but also has a completely different philosophy about how they should be treated (see Characters and Themes).

Mrs Kay is on the pupils' side: she likes them. Mr Briggs does not seem to understand them.

In his introduction to the Methuen Young Drama edition of the play, Willy Russell states that the play may be staged anywhere in the country and the setting adapted accordingly (a school in the north-east of England produced the play with the school setting in Hartlepool rather than Liverpool, the Tyne Tunnel for the Mersey Tunnel and Bamburgh Castle in Northumberland for Conway Castle in Wales). The economic and social aspects of the setting are more important to the play than the actual city in which it takes place. However, it is important for those studying the play to be aware of the language, **idiom** (see Literary Terms) and humour which are of Liverpool: further guidance will be given in the notes, commentaries and glossaries.

Part two

Summaries

General summary

Section 1 *(Act I, pp. 7–24)*	The play opens outside an inner-city school one morning, with the arrival of pupils from the 'Progress Class', the school's name for the lowest achieving group, taught by Mrs Kay. Today Mrs Kay, accompanied by two young teachers, Colin and Susan, is taking them on a day trip to Conway Castle in Wales, and they are all very excited. It becomes obvious that many of the children are from poorer homes as their parents can only let them go 'if it's free'.

Mr Briggs, one of the stricter teachers, tries to persuade the head to cancel the trip but in the end agrees to go along to keep order. Digga and Reilly, two of Mrs Kay's former pupils who are now back in normal classes, persuade her to take them along too.

When the bus arrives, the driver makes it clear that he does not approve of the Progress Class but Mrs Kay talks him into a better frame of mind and convinces him that the pupils are so deprived that he should be extra nice to them. After some jockeying for position between Digga and Reilly and the Progress Class boys, the trip gets underway, with Briggs insisting on quiet good behaviour and Mrs Kay trying to make the coach trip enjoyable. We see the bleak environment the children live in as the bus travels through Liverpool, then they go through the Mersey Tunnel singing happily. A toilet stop comes next, insisted on by Mrs Kay although Mr Briggs would happily have made the children wait.

Section 2 (Act I, pp. 24–36) This is followed by a stop at a roadside café and sweetshop. Here, the children cause chaos, stealing sweets and confusing the shopkeeper, while Mr Briggs and Mrs Kay sit outside.

Linda, one of the pupils, believes she is in love with the young teacher Colin, and she and her friend Jackie embarrass him by telling him that she thinks he is lovely. At the same time, Reilly, who is equally attracted to Susan, calls out to her and amuses his friends by showing off. Mr Briggs criticises Mrs Kay soundly to Colin, who is trying not to be drawn into conversation of this kind.

Meanwhile Mrs Kay has persuaded the driver to call in at the zoo for an hour; she disarms Mr Briggs by announcing to the children that he is an expert and that he will tell them anything they need to know about the animals. At first the zoo visit appears to be going well, with the pupils plying Mr Briggs with questions, but when he and Mrs Kay take a coffee break, the pupils get up to mischief, hiding small animals inside their coats. They are only discovered when a keeper stops the coach from leaving, and Mr Briggs becomes furious with the children, telling them that the reason no-one trusts them is that they behave like animals.

Section 3 (Act II, pp. 37–48)   On arrival at Conway Castle, Mr Briggs makes it clear that he is in charge after the zoo disaster by splitting the class into four groups and stating the time it will take each to walk round the castle with a teacher. The pupils move off and Briggs lectures his group on their lack of cultural understanding and enthusiasm for their heritage. Meanwhile Colin finds himself embarrassingly alone with Linda and Jackie who are anxious to hang upon his every word. Mrs Kay, who is talking to Carol and Andrews, two of the most deprived children, is interrupted by Briggs who berates her lack of discipline and organisation in no uncertain terms, pointing out the children running about and chasing each other instead of listening to the teachers. She responds angrily and a passionate argument follows on the purpose of education and the future opportunities for young people like the Progress Class.

The argument ends with Mrs Kay refusing to take the children home until they have visited the beach. She and the other two teachers round the children up and take them down to the sand, where some of them are overawed by the space. Some play football with the driver while Susan finally sorts out Reilly with a clever bit of bluff, and then a serious chat in which she makes him see that Linda actually likes him (which solves Colin's problem with Linda too).

Section 4 (Act II, pp. 48–58)

Meanwhile, Mrs Kay and the others have realised that Carol is missing. We see her up on the cliff top, where Mr Briggs finds her. She refuses to come down at his command, threatening to jump off the cliff if he approaches her, and explaining that she can't bear to leave the seaside and return to Liverpool. Eventually he persuades her to leave with him, they rejoin Mrs Kay, and something Carol has said to Briggs has made him think, for, surprisingly, he proposes a trip to the fair before going home.

The group enjoy themselves at the fair, Briggs most of all, before returning home on the coach. During the journey Mrs Kay completes taking photographs of the trip, and Mr Briggs offers to develop them in the school darkroom.

On arrival in Liverpool, the children leave the coach, Reilly now paired with Linda and Digga with Jackie, thanking the teachers for a lovely day. Carol is the last to leave, and watches Mr Briggs as the other three teachers go off gratefully for a drink. Unaware of her watching eyes, he deliberately exposes the film of the day out. The play ends with the children singing 'No one can take this time away' and of a parent yelling to Carol to 'get in this bloody house'.

DETAILED SUMMARIES

SECTION 1 ACT I, PAGES 7–24: (LEAVING THE INNER CITY)

The play opens with a song from the children, announcing to the audience the fact that they are going on a special day out. Carol, one of the more deprived children in the class, is introduced as she says hello to Les, the Lollipop Man. He is very old, blind and can hardly walk, asking Carol to see him back across the road. While doing so, she talks to him excitedly about the day out. She has forgotten where they are going, but tells Les that only the kids in the 'Progress Class' are to go. She explains that the Progress Class is for low achievers who cannot do the basics: reading or sums or writing, and Les expresses the opinion that Mrs Kay must be busy, as all the locals are backward.

The Progress Class makes the least progress!

As Mr Briggs approaches, Carol hurries into school, and there follows a conversation between Les and Briggs, where the Lollipop Man refuses to allow the teacher to cross the road without his assistance. Mrs Kay and the Progress Class now enter, singing about their day out, and Mrs Kay collects her class together by asking those who have not paid to come to one side: every child does so. Mr Briggs looks on disapprovingly.

The head and Briggs don't quite know how to handle Mrs Kay.

The scene changes to the head's study, where Mr Briggs questions the head as to how Mrs Kay got away with arranging the trip, when he had banned all Remedial Department outings following complaints from Derbyshire people after their last trip. The head explains that George, probably his deputy, approved it in his absence as he was not aware of the ban. Briggs tries to persuade the head to cancel the trip, but the head is reluctant in case Mrs Kay resigns, saying that she does a good job keeping the least able children busy and out of the way, and so Mr Briggs agrees to go with her instead to keep order.

Meanwhile, as Mrs Kay and the young teacher Susan
try to stop her class running into the road, two former
Progress Class pupils, Digga and Reilly, ask if they can
go. Mrs Kay says that she would willingly take them,
but that they need permission from their form teacher,
who is Mr Briggs. She tells them to get a note from
him before she will allow them to join the trip. As
Carol is asking Mrs Kay again where they are going
and she is explaining patiently that Conway in Wales is

their destination, Colin, the other young teacher
accompanying the trip, arrives, much to the delight of
Linda Croxley and her friend Jackie, who fancy him.

Notice how the
driver says he
usually does 'the
better schools'.

The coach then arrives and Mrs Kay tells the children
to board it, but she is stopped by the driver, who sings
his song 'Boss of the Bus', in which he tells the cast and
the audience what kind of a driver he is: a bossy one
who will not allow lemonade, sweets, chewing gum or
travel sickness on his vehicle. He refuses to allow the
children onto the bus until Mrs Kay has checked them
for chocolate and lemonade. Mrs Kay uses an
unexpected tactic to disarm him: she takes him to one
side and asks his name. Once she is on first-name terms
with him, she explains that the children with her are so
deprived that they do not even know what it is to taste

The bus driver is made to look silly.

chocolate and lemonade. As the two young teachers get the class onto the bus, she winds up her speech in a mock pathetic way about the children who are always 'looking and longing but never getting'. Ronnie, grief stricken, and ignorant of the fact that behind him the kids are stuffing themselves with lemonade and sweets, climbs onto the coach and gives the nearest child money to go and buy sweets for the class.

Mrs Kay announces her rule for the day: that the class are to enjoy themselves but do nothing silly or hurtful to themselves or others. She is halted by the arrival of Digga, Reilly and Mr Briggs. The two older boys immediately take possession of the best places on the back seat, while Briggs barks orders at various children and instructs them on enjoyment in his next song. They are to sit quietly, look at the scenery and behave. The child sent to buy sweets arrives as the song ends, and the driver distracts Mr Briggs by 'having a word' about the deprivation these children suffer, which makes him say as he climbs back on the coach that the driver is a 'right head-case'. Meanwhile, as the sweets are distributed by Colin and Susan, we learn from the jibes of the older boys, Digga and Reilly, that the two young teachers have been seen going out together. Reilly is jealous: he would like to take Susan out himself!

The deprived environment of the class is described.

The coach starts off on the journey, with a song from the cast letting the audience know what sort of environment the bus is travelling through; inner-city Liverpool is described: streets, houses, broken windows, the unemployed. At the end of the song, the action is focused on the back seat where Digga and Reilly light up their cigarettes, with a little kid threatening to tell on them and an older one, Andrews, begging for a cigarette. Seeing Mr Briggs approaching, Reilly quickly hands his cigarette to Andrews who takes an enormous puff, unaware of the teacher until he is well and truly caught. Briggs tells him to go to the front of the coach and himself sits between Digga and Reilly.

Several conversations now take place on different parts of the bus. Mrs Kay and Carol talk, Carol saying that she hates inner-city Liverpool and would like to live in a nice place with a garden and trees. She asks Mrs Kay wistfully if she thinks that there is any chance, if she works hard and learns to read and write, that she could be able to live somewhere like this. Briggs talks to *Reilly manages to* Reilly and Digga about the wealth of history down in *score a point* Liverpool docks, to which Reilly replies that his father, *against Briggs.* who used to work down there, hated it. When Briggs tells him to tell his father to take another look, Reilly replies that he hasn't seen him for two years.

Briggs then has an altercation with Linda, who is dressed outlandishly. She appears uncowed by his unpleasantness to her. Briggs continues to the front of the coach, telling Maurice to go to the back so that he can sit with Andrews. He lectures Andrews about smoking but the thirteen-year-old tells him that he cannot give it up. We learn a little about Andrews' home: his father is usually absent except when he wants money, when he comes round and argues with his mother.

See if you feel any The coach now approaches the Mersey Tunnel, to the *sympathy for Mr* accompaniment of another song, where twice Briggs *Briggs.* rises to his feet as he thinks the children are about to sing an obscenity, and on the third verse, when he stays seated, they sing it, loudly. After the trip through the tunnel various children ask to go to the toilet, and Briggs is all for making them wait, but Mrs Kay intervenes, saying that she would also like to go, so, defeated, Briggs asks the driver to pull in at the next toilets and all the children get off. Colin converses with the older boys, who tease him about showing Miss 'the woods' and Reilly cheekily offers to do it for him. The children climb on again and the driver sets off, with one small boy shouting that he wants the toilet as they drive away.

COMMENT In the first part of Act I we meet all the main characters (see Literary Terms) in the play and learn about the relationships between them to some extent. There is comedy (see Literary Terms) in the initial exchange between Les, the half blind Lollipop Man, and Carol, and also a wry humour and irony (see Literary Terms) in the way they talk about the Progress Class (the children who often make least progress at school or anywhere). Les gets the better of Briggs, however, and the audience enjoys a laugh at his expense; Carol has already given away the fact that the children do not like him by the way she say to Les, 'there's Briggs'. We also laugh at the officious attitude of Les 'hired' by the government and determined to do his job.

We learn that Mrs Kay and Mr Briggs have completely different attitudes to the children. Mrs Kay is determined to give her class 'a good day out', while Mr Briggs expects school outings to be run in a disciplined way and to be overtly educational. We learn that the head of the school has actually banned Mrs Kay's class from trips following a previous disaster where complaints were made to the school by residents of Derbyshire, but that she has taken advantage of the head's absence at a conference to get the permission of the deputy, George, who is unaware of the ban. This shows how determined she is to give her class a good time in that she will defy her boss and circumvent the procedures in her school to get her own way. The result is that Briggs agrees to go on the trip to keep order.

Think why the head does not simply cancel the trip. Maybe the head is worried about appearing to undermine George who has given permission, but the reason he gives Briggs is that Mrs Kay would resign if the trip were cancelled, and though Mr Briggs feels that the school would be better off without her, the head disagrees. He feels that she does a good job and keeps the least able and potentially most disruptive children safely out of the way. He seems to misunderstand the needs of these children and to feel that, as long as they are out of the way, the main business of the school can go on quite well without them. Without Mrs Kay, however, he would have to recruit another remedial teacher, which might be difficult in itself as there is a shortage of people with the right skills, but also he may have to face some truths about what these children in the Progress Class actually need at school, and that would be uncomfortable. So he agrees that the trip can go ahead with Mr Briggs keeping discipline.

Think whether either Reilly or Linda believes that there is any chance of developing a relationship with the teacher they like and admire.

The relationships between other **characters** (see Literary Terms) also become clear. Colin and Susan, the two young teachers, support Mrs Kay and what she is trying to do but lack her experience. They are just starting to go out together outside school, which has been noticed by the more streetwise pupils, who tease them about it. Reilly fancies Susan and this adds an edge to his teasing comments. Linda is also in love, with Colin, and she is as jealous of Susan as Reilly is of Colin.

We learn much about the home environment of the children in the Progress Class:
- Carol's idea of heaven is to live in a nice house with a garden, in a street with trees. The ones planted after the riots in her street were quickly vandalised and chopped down.
- Andrews rarely sees his father, who only comes round to the house when he runs out of money, and then only to row with his mother.
- Reilly has not seen his father for two years. There is a huge gulf between Briggs's appreciation of the fine

architecture at the Liverpool docks, and Reilly's view of a place which his father hated, when he had a job there.

- Most of the children cannot afford to pay for the trip and are only allowed to go if it is free.
- Many of the packed lunches they are given contain cheap ingredients like jam sandwiches, suggesting that there is not much money at home.
- The children often dislike their environment, but see no way out of it.

Think whether Mrs Kay's talk about the children left to wander the cold cruel streets is realistic and why the driver falls for it.

The bus driver is against the class at first, telling Mrs Kay that his firm is used to the 'better schools', but she convinces him that he should feel sorry for the children rather than dislike them, and he ends up firmly on their side. **Ironically** (see Literary Terms), while Mrs Kay is telling the bus driver that the children never even get a chance to look at a bar of chocolate, the children are busy munching away at their sweets.

On page 20, see if Briggs makes any impression on Linda and who seems to get the better of the exchange.

The children show obvious dismay when Mr Briggs arrives on the bus, and Mrs Kay, Susan and Colin are also displeased. Briggs immediately alienates a number of the children, in particular Linda, who is quite rude to him.

All Briggs's conversations with the kids show a lack of understanding of their world and their home environment: he expects Reilly to tell his father how grand the docks are architecturally, when it is clear that to Reilly senior the docks represented a hated workplace and now, possibly, he is unemployed. He does not know quite what to say to Andrews when he confesses that at thirteen he cannot stop smoking, and that far from hitting him to punish him for smoking, his father hits him because he refuses to share his cigarettes with him. In this exchange on pages 21–2, it becomes clear that as well as providing a lot of the play's humour, these confrontations between Briggs and the children also provide an insight into the deprivation they suffer; bleakness is combined with the laughter.

The incident where the bus stops at the toilets again illustrates the differences between Mr Briggs and Mrs Kay. He would have the children wait until they reach Wales, because this is part of his philosophy of discipline, but she refuses to ignore her own or the children's human needs and suggests a stop, possibly as a way of avoiding trouble for the entire journey. The incident also shows the difference in Colin's approach to discipline from Mr Briggs. He is too inexperienced to be able to force Reilly to put out his cigarette, but he is wise enough to avoid being confrontational when he cannot win.

GLOSSARY

Tarar (colloquial Liverpool) good-bye

tight (local dialect) mean

staccato (musical) rapped out sharply

feigned pretended

segues (musical) merges into

Corpy (abbreviation) Corporation

barney (local dialect) row, argument, fight

A *Identify the speaker.*

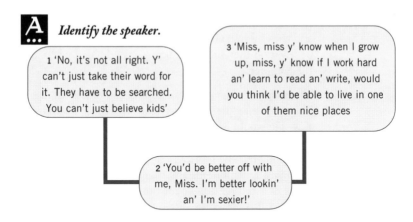

3 'Miss, miss y' know when I grow up, miss, y' know if I work hard an' learn to read an' write, would you think I'd be able to live in one of them nice places

1 'No, it's not all right. Y' can't just take their word for it. They have to be searched. You can't just believe kids'

2 'You'd be better off with me, Miss. I'm better lookin' an' I'm sexier!'

Identify the person 'to whom' this comment refers.

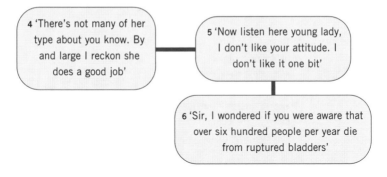

4 'There's not many of her type about you know. By and large I reckon she does a good job'

5 'Now listen here young lady, I don't like your attitude. I don't like it one bit'

6 'Sir, I wondered if you were aware that over six hundred people per year die from ruptured bladders'

Check your answers on page 79.

B *Consider these issues.*

a The role of the bus driver in this first part of the play.

b Briggs's relationships with the children and what they reveal about him, and the children's backgrounds.

c Mrs Kay's conversation with Carol and what it reveals about both of them.

SECTION 2 ACT I, PAGES 25–36: (FUN AT THE ZOO)

These songs of the bored girls are becoming a routine. Think why the author includes them.

As the coach journey progresses, two bored girls sing about how bored they are with the trip so far, with nothing to do but look at the scenery.

Mrs Kay suggests to Ronnie that they stop for a break, and he obligingly pulls up at a roadside shop and café. Mr Briggs, who is not pleased at the stop, makes the children line up outside the coach, and he and Mrs Kay express their opposing views in the song 'A straight line is a wonderful thing to behold'. While the class rushes into the shop, Mrs Kay persuades Mr Briggs to join her in having a cup of coffee out of her flask, and the scene

Consider whether the teachers should have allowed the pupils into the shop without them.

switches rapidly between the two teachers' conversation and the kids in the shop. The teachers argue, with Briggs wanting to intervene and supervise and Mrs Kay adopting a relaxed attitude to what might be going on inside the shop. Inside the shop the children are arguing with the assistants over prices, and stealing sweets whenever they can get away with it.

Back on the coach, Colin is in an embarrassing situation as Linda and Jackie both try to persuade him to sit by them, and Linda tells him how much she thinks of him. Linda sings of her love for 'Sir', which is doomed because 'Sir' is in love with Susan. Jackie taunts

Think whether Jackie is right, or whether Linda is right to hope.

her, telling her that she will marry someone just like her father, who will leave her when she has children and loses her looks, and she'll end up a single mother in a council flat.

Meanwhile Mr Briggs is trying to gain Colin's sympathy by criticising Mrs Kay's philosophy. Colin, however, supports Mrs Kay. He says that she likes the kids and that her sole concern is to give them a good day out. While this argument is taking place, the bus has turned off route. Mrs Kay has persuaded Ronnie

FUN AT THE ZOO

Consider Mrs
Kay's clever tactics
here.

that there is time to call in at the zoo for an hour, and she disarms Mr Briggs's protests by saying that first of all there is plenty of time to see Conway Castle, and then informs the children that Mr Briggs is something of a natural history expert and will tell them all they wish to know about the animals. Defeated, Briggs gets off the coach and accompanies a group of children around the zoo.

At first the zoo visit goes well, with children plying Briggs with questions and behaving well. There is an interesting conversation with Andrews and Ronson about the behaviour of captive wild animals. The two bored girls are, as usual, bored. When the children attempt to link arms with Mr Briggs he tells them to walk properly, as they meet Mrs Kay who is walking with children holding both her arms. She talks Mr

Think whether
this is a wise
decision.

Briggs into going for a cup of tea with her in the zoo café, arguing that the zoo is walled in and the two young teachers, Colin and Susan, are walking around to supervise. The children add their voices to the persuasion.

The conversation in the café is the friendliest that the two teachers have had, and Mr Briggs is genuinely surprised and impressed by the pupils' good behaviour and interest in the animals. He offers to come to the Remedial Department in his free lesson soon and show the pupils some slides of animals. When Mrs Kay and Mr Briggs leave the café, they find that Colin and Susan are with the children who are lined up and waiting to board the coach, looking innocent. Suspecting nothing, Mrs Kay begins to get them on the coach, but is interrupted by a zoo keeper who runs up roaring that the children are animals, and demanding something back which, it appears, the children have taken. At first they act innocent, but the keeper opens the jacket of one to reveal a hen, and a moment later the floodgates open, with small animals from the zoo's Pets' Corner appearing from every conceivable place. Act I ends with Briggs losing his temper with the pupils, yelling at them that he trusted them and they repaid him with such bad behaviour. He tells them that they will always be treated like animals because they behave like animals.

C OMMENT   The two scenes which take place in this part of the play, namely the visits to the shop and the zoo, not only provide a setting for the comedy (see Literary Terms) as the children get into all kinds of trouble, but also provide a vehicle for the author to express the different philosophies of Mrs Kay and Mr Briggs. The song 'Straight Line', sung as the children are getting off the coach to visit the shop, is a means of expressing the views of Briggs who wants the children 'looking tidy' and everything 'by the book', in contrast to those of Mrs Kay who accepts the children as they are, 'That's one thing they'll never look', and gently mocks Briggs with her lines, 'A straight line is a wonderful thing to behold' … 'If you stake your reputation on a stationary queue'. Briggs wants the pupils to treat the shop with the respect it deserves because the people who run the place provide a valuable service, while Mrs Kay is more

FUN AT THE ZOO

cynical about the motives of the owners, arguing with Briggs that they are only there for profit. She appears to resent the fact that the shop is making a profit from deprived children and her dragging Mr Briggs away to have coffee with her from her flask almost condones the mischief they get up to in the shop, barracking the assistants and stealing as much as they can. There is *comedy* in the quick contrasts of scene between the teachers enjoying a moment's peace with Mrs Kay's flask of coffee, and the mayhem inside the shop. Milton, as usual, is being a barrack-room lawyer, arguing about the cost of penny chews, while the other pupils steal.

Think whether it was wise of Mrs Kay to allow the children into the shop alone.

In between this incident and the visit to the zoo is the brief **interlude** (see Literary Terms) with Colin, Jackie and Linda, who is 'in love with Sir'. At one level we laugh at Colin's embarrassed discomfiture and at the antics of the two girls, but at a deeper level we are made acutely aware of the hopelessness of Linda's position and her bleak future; she is, as Jackie cynically points out, likely to repeat her mother's life, marrying a man like her father who will leave her when things become difficult or she loses her looks. Linda is likely to end up as a single parent living in poverty, as are Jackie and probably most of the girls on the coach. By contrast, Susan, of whom Linda is so jealous because she is going out with Colin, exemplifies the opportunities that the girls in the Progress Class lack, being attractive, intelligent and well educated with a career and a good-looking boyfriend of similar social and professional status. Her presence on the coach makes the girls feel hopeless (and Colin's presence has a similar effect on boys like Digga and Reilly though they express it rather differently).

Consider who has the audience's sympathy here: Colin, Susan or Linda.

At the zoo, events take an unexpected turn when the children show their interest and enthusiasm and ask Mr

Briggs lots of questions. The conversation at the bear pit is a significant one in the development of the play because in many ways it **symbolises** (see Literary Terms) what is going on in the lives of the pupils and of Mr Briggs. He accepts the *status quo*, that in Britain we have zoos and that it is generally considered acceptable to keep potentially dangerous animals like bears in pits, and he comments that the animal will not know any other sort of existence. The children, however, challenge his view, with Ronson saying that being in captivity may actually create the bear's viciousness. A girl disagrees with him, supporting Briggs's views. The argument mirrors that of Carol and Andrews with Mrs Kay in Act II, where Andrews argues that if Conway Castle belonged to the children they would look after it and defend it rather than vandalise it, while Carol maintains that no-one will ever give children like her anything to look after because they would just destroy it. These conversations are **symbolic** of the children themselves; they are like the brown bears, imprisoned by their class, their environment and their lack of ability, and there is a question for the audience to consider: is society in danger if we set these children free? Mr Briggs would certainly 'imprison' them and keep them in their place in society, while Mrs Kay feels that their traditional 'place' has gone for ever, and that no-one quite knows where these children and others like them fit in any more.

Consider what Willy Russell is saying about the children's lives through the 'brown bear' conversation.

Consider why the children don't fit into society any more.

Mr Briggs is pleasantly surprised and appears to be revising his judgements of them and becoming more sympathetic to Mrs Kay when they talk in the café. This makes the contrast between his later behaviour, when the extent of the children's naughtiness is discovered, all the more effective. Both audience and readers will laugh heartily as the slapstick **comedy** (see

Literary Terms) takes place of the irate zoo keeper forcing the children to yield up the small animals they have 'borrowed', but the serious message is delivered at the **climax** (see Literary Terms) of Act I a minute later when Briggs launches into his furious tirade against the children, calling them 'animals' and the Act ends on a sombre note.

GLOSSARY   *apoplectic* furious, almost ready to burst with anger

surcharge charge added on just for school parties

Trades Description Act law stating that goods sold in shops must be described accurately and not in a way which would mislead the customer

liberalism attitude or belief in which freedom of expression is important rather than conforming to rules

sarnies (colloquial) sandwiches

Evertonian supporter of Everton football team, traditional rival of Liverpool Football Club

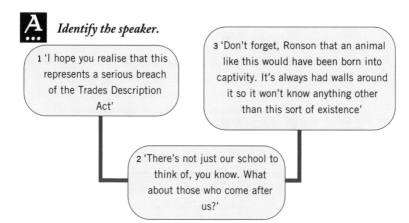

A *Identify the speaker.*

1 'I hope you realise that this represents a serious breach of the Trades Description Act'

3 'Don't forget, Ronson that an animal like this would have been born into captivity. It's always had walls around it so it won't know anything other than this sort of existence'

2 'There's not just our school to think of, you know. What about those who come after us?'

Identify the person 'to whom' this comment refers.

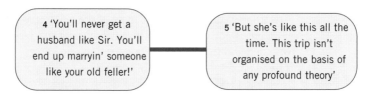

4 'You'll never get a husband like Sir. You'll end up marryin' someone like your old feller!'

5 'But she's like this all the time. This trip isn't organised on the basis of any profound theory'

Check your answers on page 79.

B *Consider these issues.*

a Who is right about discipline, lining up, respect etc.: Mr Briggs or Mrs Kay and who gets the sympathy of the audience.

b Consider the conversation between Briggs and the children on page 33. What does it tell you about his attitude and theirs? Think whether it makes you think about the children's environment.

c Think whether the teachers should have left the pupils unsupervised in the shop or in the zoo and what the consequences are.

d Say what you think of Mr Briggs's attitude at the end of Act I.

SECTION **3** ACT II, PAGES 37–48: (FREEDOM)

At the beginning of Act II the party arrive at Conway Castle. Mr Briggs takes charge, splitting the children into four groups and determining how long it will take for each group to tour the castle with a teacher. He moves off with his group, who are not enthusiastic as they were about the animals, and begins explaining the finer points of past military strategy to them. He accuses them, when they tell him that the castle is boring, of being bored because they fail to invest in anything and therefore get nothing in return. Digga and Reilly slip away from his group in order to have a smoke.

Think whether the boys should have paid more attention. Consider the reasons for their lack of interest.

Meanwhile Colin, in whose group Linda and Jackie have contrived to be, has lost most of the children with him, but is pursued enthusiastically by Linda and Jackie who demand that he tell them everything he knows. They again embarrass him by pretending to be frightened and throwing their arms round him, a situation which is worsened by Digga and Reilly creeping up behind the girls to touch them and scare them.

Meanwhile Mrs Kay has given up on educating the pupils about the castle and is sitting on the battlements talking to Carol, who thinks the sea is a lake, and Andrews. They tell her that they have no decent facilities for play at home in Liverpool, but Andrews suggests that if they were given a facility like this castle, they would defend and look after it. Carol is not convinced. At this point in their conversation they are interrupted by Mr Briggs, who tells the children to go as he wants to talk to Mrs Kay. Defeated, they leave.

Mrs Kay begins by being angry with Briggs for driving away the children with whom she was talking, and he

Think who has your sympathy during this argument, Mr Briggs or Mrs Kay, and why.

launches into a furious tirade against her lack of discipline and the way in which the children, who are by now chasing each other joyfully round the castle ruins, are left to their own devices. He sees the outcome of the trip as chaos; she sees it as children freed from the restraints of school and having a good time. A serious row, one of the real **climaxes** (see Literary Terms) of the play, now follows, in which Mrs Kay passionately defends her strategies for making things a bit better for society's rejects, while Briggs disagrees with almost everything she says. The argument ends with Briggs threatening to take charge and order the children home immediately, but Mrs Kay counters his words by announcing that they are going down to the beach instead.

The children are delighted to be taken to the beach, and sing of the freedom and the various things they can do. For most of them the beach is a new experience. Ronnie arranges a game of football with some of them. Meanwhile Carol is worrying about having to go home, to the extent that she does not seem to be enjoying the visit as she should, despite Mrs Kay's encouragement.

Think why Mrs Kay cannot answer Carol's question.

Mrs Kay eventually has to tell her that this is a special day and that things cannot be like this all the time, but she has no answer to Carol's question 'why not?' The bored girls refuse to play football because it's boring, though they like it on the television.

Reilly continues to taunt Susan as she and Colin examine the rock pools with some of the girls, including, inevitably, Linda and Jackie. Colin begins to tell Reilly off but says to Susan that he feels he cannot get through to the boy. Susan wonders aloud whether she could, and goes to try a strategy of her own on him. Linda, asking Colin whether Susan is going to sort out Reilly, tells him that he is really different when on his own, away from the friends before whom he shows off.

Think whether Susan's strategy was wise and could it have gone wrong.

Susan calls Reilly's bluff, pretending to be all his in a comic scene. Reilly is truly terrified and backs down into the youngster he really is. Susan, after making her point and telling him to drop the act, asks him whether he has ever thought about Linda as a potential girlfriend. Reilly at first dismisses the idea, saying that she would not be interested in him because of her crush on Colin, but in a song Susan puts the case for Linda and ends by persuading Reilly that it would be worth asking her out. One of the comic elements in this scene is that, at the time Susan is pretending to be flirting with Brian Reilly, she is observed by Mr Briggs, who completely misinterprets what is going on.

Meanwhile the action returns to the football match on the beach, where Mrs Kay says she is too tired to continue in goal and looks around for Carol to replace her. It becomes apparent that no-one has seen Carol for some time, and Mrs Kay, Colin and Susan are quite worried. When Mr Briggs arrives they ask if he has seen her but he simply accuses them of being careless enough to lose her, threatening all three of them that when they get back to school they are finished professionally. He reveals that he has seen the scene between Susan and Reilly. Mrs Kay dismisses his threats by saying that the most important thing is to find Carol, and while Susan supervises the football match with Ronnie, the other three teachers go off to try and find her.

COMMENT   Briggs is firmly in control at the beginning of Act II, in response to the behaviour of the children at the zoo. However, his formal tour of the castle proves unworkable given the low ability of the pupils and their sense of wonder at being in such a different environment. They gradually drop out of the talk and revert to chasing and running around the ruins, using it as a giant adventure playground.

Mr Briggs once again expresses his lack of understanding of the world of the children. He is a history enthusiast, and cannot understand why they are not interested in the castle ruins. He also feels that the lack of interest is their fault; they invest in nothing, so will get nothing back. He deplores their telling him that the Americans have Disneyland when he says that they have nothing to compare with the historic castle.

See who you think is right: Andrews, who claims that they would look after things, or Carol who disagrees.

His enthusiasm should infect them, but he is so detached from their world that he appears pompous and remote in their eyes and his message fails to come across. The conversation between Carol, Andrews and Mrs Kay shows how vulnerable these two children are but also poses some questions about the environment and facilities for recreation experienced by these young people.

When Briggs interrupts, it clearly does not signify with him that Mrs Kay's conversation with the two children matters at all. Her quiet dignified reminder that she was talking to those children has him at a loss, and he resorts to bluster and to telling her off as if she were one of the children. The conversation which follows is the heart of the play. Mr Briggs relies on the attitudes which have always carried him through his teaching career, refusing to admit that the children in the Progress Class might have any special needs which render his approach irrelevant or inadequate. He sees Mrs Kay's being on their side as a serious fault. Mrs Kay's attitudes are in many ways understandable. For years she has worked to the best of her ability with the children at the bottom of the pile and she is sometimes near to despair about the lack of opportunities for them. She blames society for rejecting them and for there being no longer anything for them to do: the unskilled labour that such children once provided when they left school is now no longer needed. Her attitude is that at least she can try to make things a little better for them by giving them a good day out and showing them that she cares for them. She realises that she can do nothing to change the situation, but that at least she can try to give them some fun which they may remember.

On the other hand, Briggs refuses to consider any child as a failure. He wants to treat the Progress Class as he would treat any pupils, expecting high standards of behaviour and work from them. He does not believe that the day out should be for fun, but that they should be learning about the castle. He is contemptuous of Mrs Kay's views and accuses her of having the wrong attitude for a member of the teaching profession.

Mr Briggs takes 'professionalism' very seriously.

Carol, perhaps the most deprived child in the class, is badgering Mrs Kay because she does not want to accept that she must go home. Mrs Kay comes closer than she ever has to being honest with her when she admits that she cannot give her an answer to her question, 'Why can't it always be like this?' We sense at the end of this section that Carol is heading for trouble.

The interplay between Susan and Brian Reilly is comic because it develops the **stereotypical** (see Literary

Consider whether Linda and Reilly are well suited.

Terms) story of boy in love with teacher, but in an unexpected way Susan neatly turns the tables on Reilly by calling his bluff, pretending that she has taken him seriously. Alarmed, he drops his act and is ready to respond to her serious talk in which she suggests that Linda is perhaps a more suitable girlfriend for a boy his age. By planting this idea in his mind she also solves Colin's problem with Linda's teenage 'crush'. Unexpected **comedy** (see Literary Terms) is provided by the fact that Briggs witnesses the scene between Susan and Reilly and completely misinterprets it. He imagines that what he sees as the permissiveness of Mrs Kay's attitudes extends to the behaviour of the younger staff with the pupils.

This part of the play ends with the discovery, half expected by the audience, that Carol is missing. Mr Briggs is unsurprised as he expects Mrs Kay to lose half her pupils, but the others are concerned that some harm has come to her.

GLOSSARY

battlements defensive part of a castle

goalie (colloquial) goalkeeper

A *Identify the speaker.*

1 'Bored? Yes, and you'll be bored forever ... Because you put nothing in! You invest in nothing'

3 'We bring them out to a crumbling pile of bricks and mortar and they think they're in the fields of heaven'

2 'That's why we never have nothin' nice round our way – we'd smash it up'

Identify the person 'to whom' this comment refers.

4 'You'll never teach them because nobody knows what to do with them'

5 'Now you listen to me ... you're a handsome lad, but I suggest that in future you stay in your own league ...'

Check your answers on page 79.

B *Consider these issues.*

a Look again at the argument between Mrs Kay and Mr Briggs on pages 41 and 42, and decide whose arguments you agree with.

b Carol asks Mrs Kay why every day cannot be like the day out. Think why Mrs Kay makes the reply she does.

c Consider the way in which Susan deals with Reilly.

Section **4** Act II, pages 49–58:
(CRISIS FOR CAROL AND RETURN JOURNEY)

*Think whether
Carol's behaviour
is in character and
why she defies Mr
Briggs.*

While Susan keeps the rest of the children playing
football with Ronnie, Mrs Kay, Mr Briggs and Colin
split up to search for Carol. The audience is shown the
girl on a lonely cliff top, contemplating the sea and the
town, and wondering why, as she asked Mrs Kay, it
can't always be this way. She sings a song expressing
her wish that she could freeze this moment and keep it
for ever. Just then Briggs discovers her, yelling at her to
leave the cliffs at once. Carol, wrought up with
emotion, defies him, which makes him angrier. She
threatens to jump over the cliff if he comes near her.
When he tries to persuade her, seeing that threats and
shouting are having no effect, she accuses him of not
caring about her or the children like her. Briggs softens
in his attitude, and persuades her gently to come with
him, pulling her back from the edge of the cliff as she
slips.

Meanwhile Mrs Kay and the young teachers are on the
point of reporting Carol as missing to the police, when
she and Briggs return to the beach. He orders everyone
back onto the coach and the driver assumes that the trip
is over, but to everyone's surprise and delight Briggs

suggests a visit to the fair before going home. The fairground is set up on stage to the accompaniment of a song describing the fun the group has on the dodgems, the waltzer and the ghost train, with Briggs posing for photographs in a 'kiss-me-quick' hat, at the finale of the song.

The pupils then reassemble the coach as they sing a typical coach trip song, 'Everywhere we go'. They climb aboard, and we see that Linda and Reilly are partners, as are Digga and Jackie. Mrs Kay continues to take photographs of the happy group as the children sing, 'She'll be coming round the mountain' to represent time passing on the journey home. As most of the pupils fall asleep, Briggs seems to return to normality, removing his silly hat and placing it on Carol's head. When Mrs Kay tells him that she will put one of her photographs of the day he enjoyed himself on the staffroom notice board, he offers to develop the film in the school laboratory and she hands it over. Reilly tells Linda that this will be his last school trip as he is leaving school, and in reply to her question about what he will do, says 'nothing, I suppose'.

Consider how the 'return to normal life' is shown in this part of the play.

Arriving in Liverpool, the children wake up and climb off the bus, thanking their teachers and saying that even Briggs is not so bad. The two bored girls leave, saying how great the day was. Carol is last to leave, with Ronnie joking about pythons as he hands her her goldfish from the fair. Mrs Kay, Colin and Susan head gratefully for the pub, but Mr Briggs declines their invitation, saying he has marking to do.

Watched by Carol and the other pupils, Briggs discovers the completed film of the day in his pocket and deliberately exposes it to the light. We hear a parent's voice yelling at Carol to get inside the house. The play ends as Briggs walks off, with a song from the pupils who are left onstage, singing that no-one can take this time away, even though there are no pictures left. Their feelings about it will remain.

COMMENT We have been given some indication earlier in the play that Carol was determined to question her place in the order of things, and her running away from the group to be alone on the cliff top **symbolises** (see Literary Terms) her desperate attempt to challenge her fate as one of life's no-hopers. The **pathos** (see Literary Terms) of her song is all the more poignant because we know that she of all the children is the least capable of looking out for herself and cannot read or write.

When Mr Briggs discovers Carol, we see the enormous gulf between his world and that of the Progress Class. He confronts her aggressively, yelling at her to come back from the cliffs, and is furious when she defies him. His remark that he will not put up with 'a pile of silliness from the likes of you' is telling, because it indicates just how low in the human pecking order Briggs judges the remedial class to be. His anger and near-contempt for Carol is replaced by bewilderment when he begins to realise how serious her threat is to jump off the cliff if he does not leave her alone. He asks her what she is trying to do, but at this point Carol does not appear to know. She is overwrought, desperate and at the same time strangely perceptive

Think how at this point Briggs's attitude appears to change.

when she declares that Briggs is scared of being in trouble if she jumps. She points out bluntly to him the difference between their worlds when she describes his attitude to the pupils as he drives past every day in his car.

Consider whether she has anything to look forward to in the future.

Briggs tells Carol that it sounds as if, for her, life is ending rather than beginning.

Carol's response to Briggs when he exhorts her to work hard, get a good job and move out to Wales when she is older is one of pure contempt. In a sentence she dismisses him and all he stands for. At the same time, she begins to calm down and realise that the stance she has taken is hopeless and that she cannot stay in Conway. She also realises how much her background has influenced her opportunities, when she says that if Briggs had been her father she would have been all right. Briggs softens towards her and gently encourages her to back away from the cliff edge, promising that she will not get into trouble for her escapade. Deciding to believe him, she edges towards his outstretched hand and almost falls, but he pulls her towards him in a dramatic climax (see Literary Terms) to the scene and stands holding onto her.

At this point, consider whether Mr Briggs may change his attitude to the Progress Class.

To the surprise of Mrs Kay and the others, Briggs makes no fuss when he and Carol return to the group on the beach, and in a dramatic about-face, suggests a visit to the fair. In the fairground scene we see that Briggs seems to have undergone a dramatic transformation to genial supporter of the children, taking them on various rides, eating ice cream and candy floss, and posing for photographs with the pupils wearing a 'kiss-me-quick' hat. There is comedy (see Literary Terms) in this transformation because it is so sudden, but the underlying message is perhaps that he has learned something during the play about the lives of the pupils and their sad lack of opportunity, which has taught him compassion for them.

Consider the sudden transformation of Mr Briggs during the fairground scenes, and whether it will last.

The music and actions towards the end of the fairground incident, as the children re-form the coach onstage and board it singing, 'Everywhere we go' and 'She'll be coming round the mountain' is highly stylised (see Literary Terms), to suggest the passing of time (see Structure). Gradually, as the children fall asleep, and we are shown the two couples, Linda and Reilly, Jackie and Digga, happily sitting together, Briggs appears to return

When Briggs offers to develop the film for Mrs Kay, think whether he intends to do so.

to normality. He becomes conscious of the silly hat and gets rid of it, straightening his tie, and seems perturbed when Mrs Kay threatens to put up a photograph of him at the fair in the staffroom.

Getting off the bus in Liverpool, the children express their surprise at Briggs's change of heart, summed up by Reilly as he walks Linda home. An extra bit of comedy of manners is provided by the two bored girls, who get off, leading the audience to expect comments about the 'boring' day, and immediately say that it was great!

The teachers disperse gratefully to the pub after bidding goodbye to Ronnie the driver. It is then that we see that Briggs's conversion has not been permanent. He refuses a drink as he has marking to do, and immediately the other three staff are offstage, he reaches into his pocket for his keys, and pulling out the film deliberately exposes it to the light in a symbolic (see Literary Terms) gesture which appears to wipe away all he has learned on the day out.

Consider whether Mr Briggs has learned anything.

We then hear Carol's parent yelling profanely at her to get in the house, a stark reminder that we are back in inner-city Liverpool, and that as Mrs Kay said in Act II, a day out was not going to change anything for these children. The resigned way in which the pupils watch Briggs's action with the film seems to underline this. However, the play ends on a note of hope as the children sing their last song, a reprise (see Literary Terms) of 'We had a really great day out' with the words 'No-one can take this time away' and the sentiments that pictures may fade or become lost but the feelings will remain for ever. They form a tableau (see Literary Terms) past which Briggs has to walk as they sing.

Think whether anything has changed for the Progress Class.

CRISIS FOR CAROL AND RETURN JOURNEY

Some editions of the play end with the yell from Carol's parent to get inside the house, with the stage being darkened immediately afterwards.

GLOSSARY   **old feller** (colloquial) father
kiss-me-quick fairground hat with silly motto designed to be fun
cracker (colloquial) great, superb

Identify the speaker.

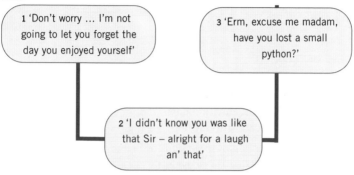

1 'Don't worry ... I'm not going to let you forget the day you enjoyed yourself'

3 'Erm, excuse me madam, have you lost a small python?'

2 'I didn't know you was like that Sir – alright for a laugh an' that'

Identify the person 'to whom' this comment refers.

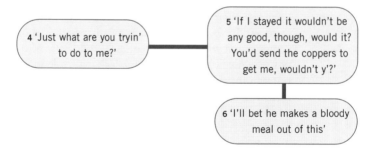

4 'Just what are you tryin' to do to me?'

5 'If I stayed it wouldn't be any good, though, would it? You'd send the coppers to get me, wouldn't y'?'

6 'I'll bet he makes a bloody meal out of this'

Check your answers on page 79.

 Consider these issues.

a Think what effect Carol's escapade on the cliffs has on Briggs and if it lasts.

b Consider how the problems of Susan and Colin have been solved by the end of the play.

c Think about how the ending, with the stage going dark as soon as Carol walks off, would change the mood at the end of the play, and which ending would be more optimistic and why.

PART THREE

COMMENTARY

THEMES

SOCIAL DEPRIVATION

The main theme in *Our Day Out* is the waste of talent and lack of opportunity among young people in socially deprived environments. The pupils in the Progress Class are without hope for the future.

Lack of basic skills

Their lack of basic skills of literacy and numeracy means that they have little chance of passing any examinations in a world where the prospect of getting any employment increasingly depends on having some qualifications.

Lack of male role models

For many of the pupils, their home circumstances dominate their lives and make it difficult for them to learn. Andrews, whose father is mostly absent and only comes round when he wants money, and Reilly who has not seen his father for two years, lack male role models to teach them how to live as men in their society. The man with whom they have most contact is Mr Briggs, but his experience of life is so far away from theirs and his attitudes so different that they cannot relate to him. The children for the most part live in homes where there is little money, no books or parental support for education; often there is only one parent who is too busy struggling to keep food on the table to worry about anything beyond the basic human needs of the children. Many are inadequately clothed or fed; jam sandwiches are the norm on the trip, and they can only go if there is nothing to pay.

The inner city

The environment of inner-city Liverpool is portrayed in bleak realism (see Literary Terms): animals running around unheeded, broken windows, derelict property,

queues for social security, of unemployed workers clad
in ragged clothes. Trees which were planted after the
riots were immediately vandalised, as is anything
provided by the council. Growing up in this
environment, for the least able children who cannot
master basic skills, leaves them no option but to join
the dole queue.

VITALITY OF YOUTH

The children's cheeky optimism is endearing.

Another theme which runs through the play is that of
the unquenchable zest and vitality of youth, and it is
this which saves the play from being oversentimental or
sad, and makes it a genuine comedy (see Literary
Terms). We laugh affectionately at the cheek and
mischief of the children, even though some of their
antics border on the criminal, for example, stealing
sweets in the shop. The cheeky optimism of Reilly, the
yearning of Linda for Sir, the jauntiness of Milton who
has an answer for everything, all are funny and endear
the characters (see Literary Terms) to the audience.
They are realistic, lively children; they cheer and shout
on the bus, tear around the castle, and play football and
ride at the fair with the enthusiasm of childhood. What
makes the play all the more poignantly sad, even as we
are laughing at the pupils' antics, is that this day almost
represents childhood's end for them. It is Reilly's last
trip, and in many ways the last chance for the Progress
Class, if only because the head teacher will certainly see
that there are no further outings for Mrs Kay and her
class, as the audience has been aware since the first Act.

Consider the contrast between the bleak surroundings and the children's liveliness.

In contrast to their bleak prospects, the children are
shown by the writer as having exuberance,
determination, wit and a zest for life. The incidents
within the day out are presented as a glorious romp,
with humour and warmth. They are passionately

interested in the animals, delighted by the freedom of running around the castle and the beach, and thrilled by the fair. Let out of school, the joys of being young and alive are clearly conveyed. Even the wrong that they do – stealing sweets, lying, 'borrowing' the animals, racing around the castle like dogs off the leash – is shown with warmth and humour and leaves us in no doubt whose

Think whether side the author is on. Their teenage crushes on the
Willy Russell is on young teachers point up their depressing prospects:
their side, even 'You'll never get a husband like Sir', but also portray
when they do with the same warmth the agony and delight of first
wrong. unrequited love for someone older and unattainable.

Education's opposing views

Education, and its role in changing life chances, is another important theme in the play. In particular the adult argument which underpins the play is presented through the ongoing conflict between Mrs Kay and Mr Briggs. There are two views of education as it applies to deprived, less able children which seem to be explored in this drama.

The liberal The first view, clearly held by Mrs Kay and supported
view to a great extent by Colin and Susan who are being trained very much in her image, is that of sympathy for the children as human beings above all else, and of liberalism. Mrs Kay respects the children, addresses them gently and politely by their first names, and treats them with the same politeness an adult would receive. She is clear about the prospects in store for them, and tries to alleviate the hardships they suffer by giving them a good time, trips out, and by bending the rules of the school in deference to their circumstances; nothing is said to Linda about wearing her own clothes because it might spoil her day out. Mrs Kay genuinely likes the pupils as people, recognising their warmth, humour and

zest for life, and feels genuine pity for them and their bleak future. She tries to compensate for its bleakness by giving them a good time, and some self-esteem and self-confidence while they are in her care. She never stands on her dignity or hides behind the role of a teacher with them, but nevertheless attempts to instil in them some care and respect for others as well as self-respect. Her expectations of their achievement are, however, low. In one sense she has already given up on these children; she clearly expects them to achieve nothing in the academic sense. She is, in the view of the head teacher, keeping them out of everyone else's way so that the real business of education can continue in the rest of the school with the most potentially disruptive children removed from classes. They are in a backwater of the school, allowed to go where they wish as long as their behaviour does not cause problems.

Mrs Kay respects the children but expects little of them.

Mr Briggs represents on the surface a more traditional view of education. He is the strictest teacher, who expects children to fall silent when adults speak, to respect authority, wear uniform, conform and work hard whatever their ability. He does not relate to the children as people, seeing them as behaviour problems to be controlled, and barking orders at them in almost military fashion. His experience is totally removed from theirs; he drives out of the inner-city environment of the school every night in his car, leaving the children's world behind him. He would certainly not allow the Progress Class out of school because he appears to think that trips out are only for polite, clever and hardworking children.

The traditional view

Mr Briggs lacks understanding of the children but has high expectations of them.

However, in another sense, the view of education represented by Briggs is more rigorous and positive. He expects the same standards of children whatever their background, refusing to make allowances or excuses for failure to reach high standards. He ignores social deprivation and believes in the power of hard work. In one sense, we could argue that Mrs Kay's approach, though it appears to be kind, is actually rather patronising ('There, there, dear, you've got learning difficulties and a poor home so I shan't expect very much of you'). Briggs, however, expects the best from all children. He demands that an educational visit for this type of child needs to be more, not less structured, and that it should have clear aims for learning and contribute to their education. In this sense it is Mrs Kay's attitude which seems the more cynical of the two when she tells him that he is in a job which is 'designed and funded to fail' because society no longer knows what to do with its unskilled young people.

Consider whom you find the more sympathetic and whom you agree with.

The author does not, however, portray Briggs as sympathetic. His complete inability to relate to the environment and background of the children is often illustrated: in the comments to Andrews about smoking, to Reilly and Digga about the docks, to Carol about working hard when she is on the cliffs. Carol clearly wins the confrontation on the cliffs and Briggs is forced to change his attitude, but the fact that the change is only temporary shows that the author's sympathy appears to lie with Carol and not Briggs. But the argument between the two teachers in Act II, where they both speak passionately and with conviction, points up for the audience the complex nature of the problem and the fact that there are no easy solutions. We are presented with both sides and to some extent left to think and make up our own minds.

STRUCTURE

Episodic structure

The structure of *Our Day Out* is episodic (see Literary Terms), telling the story of the day chronologically from beginning to end in two Acts. Incidents, events and the interplay between **characters** (see Literary Terms) blend seamlessly into each other, with the only definite break between the two Acts being between the visit to the zoo, which ends with the **climax** (see Literary Terms) of the children being discovered with the animals by the zoo keeper and called animals by Briggs, and the castle visit which begins Act II, where Briggs has clearly taken control of the day out.

The songs

The play was originally written as a television script without the songs, but in 1983 it was rewritten for the stage as a show with music. The songs in *Our Day Out* are therefore an integral part of the text as it now stands, and are interwoven with the dramatic narrative to introduce or develop **characters** (see Literary Terms), highlight crucial events and **climaxes** in the story or sometimes to indicate the passing of time or to set a scene descriptively, where the staging will not permit the scene to be presented **realistically** (see Literary Terms).

Examples of each use of songs are as follows:
- 'Boss of the Bus' is used to introduce Ronnie as a **character**, and to highlight his attitude to the type of children the Progress Class represent ('we normally do the better schools').

Songs often suggest time passing or create a scene which would be hard to stage.
- 'We're off' which leads into 'Look at the dogs' is used to indicate the passing of time as the coach sets off and travels through inner-city Liverpool, and also to describe the scene through which the children travel, telling the audience more about the setting of the school and the deprived backgrounds of the children.
- 'I'm in love with Sir' tells us more about the **character** of Linda and the prospects of girls like Linda and Jackie.

- 'Straight Line' indicates crucial differences in the way Mrs Kay and Mr Briggs treat the children, and prepares us for the events in the café and shop.
- 'Why can't it always be this way' sung by Carol on page 48, highlights the dramatic **climax** of Act II when Carol runs away and is found on the cliffs by Mr Briggs.
- 'Everywhere we go' and 'Coming Round the Mountain' are used in a highly **stylised** (see Literary Terms) way, to represent dramatically the journey home, which would otherwise be difficult onstage. In performance, the actors use benches to re-form the coach as they sing 'Everywhere we go', and climb aboard to sing a typical song, which the audience can

Songs show the audience parts of the journey which would be difficult to recreate on stage.

associate with coach outings. The way in which it is sung allows the audience to notice the developments which have taken place at the end of the day trip. Brian Reilly is now paired off with Linda, and his friend Digga with her friend Jackie. Briggs is sitting with a group of children much as Mrs Kay was on the outward journey. The song ends with the taking of the last photograph, which **symbolises** (see Literary Terms) a return to reality for Mr Briggs.

Contrast

Throughout the play, there are contrasting scenes which show the exuberance and joy of the pupils and their antics, followed almost immediately by scenes which highlight the deprivation of the children and the bleakness of their lives. Laughter and sadness are closely related in this drama. The adult argument of the dispute between Mr Briggs and Mrs Kay on the best way to educate these children or at least to make their lives better is present throughout, but is never allowed to dominate the fun the audience gets from seeing the children in action.

CHARACTERS

MRS KAY

Tolerant and kind hearted

Humorous and genuine

Compassionate and prepared to make allowances for the pupils

Mrs Kay is a liberal and open-minded teacher who is, above all, fond of the children as people. She does not regard her pupils as vessels to be filled with facts and learning, but as human beings. She is tolerant of her pupils' failings, and makes allowances for their deprived background and learning difficulties in all her dealings with them. Her attitude towards them is protective; she tells Maurice to come away from the road, when they are waiting for the bus, out of genuine concern for his safety, not because she enjoys ordering her class around. All her rules are derived from common sense rather than from any sense of a need for rules or discipline by itself.

In many ways Mrs Kay does not accept the traditional teacher role with its emphasis on discipline and high standards, and on being the boss. She tries to persuade the children to call her Helen instead of Mrs Kay, and seems surprised when the children, brought up as they are in a tough school, have difficulty with the idea. In the argument with Briggs in Act II, where she declares passionately that Briggs will not succeed in teaching her class anything because nobody knows what to do with children like this, she may seem cynical, and in some ways she is, showing a weariness with the system and the way in which it has let her pupils down. In some ways, however, she is an innocent, who cannot understand, though she is bleakly aware of, the ways in which the dice are loaded against the pupils in the Progress Class. She therefore falls back on the warm human relationship she has with these children, in seeing and treating them as people with rights and, above all, the right to respect. Perhaps this is because, being a genuine and warm-hearted human being who is at a loss to comprehend the injustice of a society which relegates these children to the back of the queue, she does not know how else to treat them. She argues that as they are not going to solve the complex problems of unequal opportunity and social injustice, at least they can give the children a good day out.

Mrs Kay seems possessed of limitless patience with the pupils. She recognises that most teachers would be impatient with Carol, who repeats the same question about where they are going again and again, possibly because she cannot keep an idea in her head for longer than a couple of minutes. However, she answers Carol's repeated questions with tolerance and cannot bring herself to say anything which may destroy the girl's slender hope of a future where she could live in 'one of them nice places'. She defends the pupils' right to personal respect, arguing with Briggs who orders Andrews and Carol to disappear so that he can talk to her. Her quiet dignified reply to him, 'I was talking to those children' awards them all the respect she thinks they deserve.

Mrs Kay often handles people cleverly: she knows how to negotiate.

Mrs Kay can be quite adept at handling and negotiating with people: the way in which she gets Ronnie the driver on her side is played for **comedy** (see Literary Terms), but it is quite effective, and she generally handles Briggs with gentle humour, often sidestepping his more rigid demands. She avoids confrontation by, for example, stopping for toilets when the children ask, and arranging a short break at the shop before they have a chance to get too bored and start making trouble. The way in which she manipulates Mr Briggs at the start of the zoo visit suggests that she does employ a little basic psychology in her way of negotiating with people.

Mrs Kay is not afraid of physical contact with the pupils; she holds hands, puts her arm round them and cuddles them when they need it, as a mother would. Indeed for many of the children she seems to have taken on the role of the good mother that perhaps they lack at home, and this has superseded her teacher role, perhaps because it is needed more. Colin remarks to Briggs that he doesn't think that the day out is organised on the basis of any philosophy of education, but merely to give the kids a good day, because she likes them. In today's more rigorous view of teaching and learning and the aims of education, Mrs Kay would probably be found wanting in several areas:

- In her lack of high expectations of pupils, and her willingness to make allowances for them.
- In her lack of planning for learning (a good day out would not be accepted as a lesson objective within the National Curriculum).
- In her lack of discipline, allowing the pupils to bring the school into disrepute by running wild on a school visit.

In her favour, however, are the following points:

- She listens to and respects pupils, according them the same dignity as adults. Thus they behave more reasonably with her.
- She genuinely cares about the pupils, and wants to make life better for them by trying to compensate for what they lack.
- She is human, with an infectious sense of fun.
- She stands by what she believes in and defends her pupils against unreasonable attitudes based on prejudice.

MR BRIGGS

Mr Briggs is almost a perfect contrast or foil for Mrs Kay. He is a traditional teacher of the 'old school' with rigorous views of discipline, standards, uniform, and appropriate work and behaviour. His traditional methods mostly ignore or sidestep the needs of the Progress Class with whom he does not really know how

Strict and
intolerant
Disciplinarian
and bossy
Rigid in attitudes
Expects very high
standards
whatever the
ability or
background of
pupils

to cope. He sees no reason to treat his pupils as human beings, being more concerned with the imparting of knowledge, and his expectations of behaviour and standards. He takes a strict line always, making the children sit quietly in their seats on the bus, telling them that they must wait until the bus reaches its destination to go to the toilet, and expecting them to line up outside the shop and walk round the castle in a controlled group. He plans a day trip like a military operation, with so many minutes allowed for each section, and is disconcerted when the bus turns unexpectedly off at the shop and the zoo.

Briggs has high expectations of the pupils. He expects them to pay attention, work hard and behave, whatever their background or ability. He shows contempt for the way in which Mrs Kay makes allowances for the pupils, and criticises her organisation and planning. His attitudes are, however, totally rigid, and he has no idea of the deprivation suffered by some of the children, seeing it as irrelevant. When he lectures Digga and Reilly on the architectural features of the docks, it is obvious that he has never spared a thought for the perspective of Reilly senior who had to work there, and he is completely nonplussed by Andrews's declaration that his father beats him up, not because he smokes but because he will not share his cigarettes! Carol has noticed the way he looks at her and the other deprived, less able children as he drives his car away from the school at night, and claims that it is with hatred. At the very least, he seems to dislike the children who do not and cannot conform to his expectations of model pupils.

In the scene with Carol on the cliff top, we recognise that Briggs is totally out of touch with the world of Carol and children like her, and we also see the arrogance which characterises some of his dealings with the pupils, when he declares that he will not put up with 'a pile of silliness from the likes of you'. (Would he be more willing to tolerate a similar outburst of hysteria from a highly strung and very clever girl, from an affluent home, we wonder.) He is not used to being challenged by the less able children, whom he drills rather as if they were foot soldiers in the army.

Briggs has high ideals but he lacks realism in his attitude to the children.

In many ways, Briggs is an idealist. He tells Mrs Kay in their argument in Act II that her attitude is unacceptable for a member of the teaching profession, and to some extent he is driven by his sense of professionalism. He believes that a stimulating day out must be totally organised and planned in terms of what the children will learn. He will not allow for any spontaneity nor indiscipline. However, there are no complaints about bad behaviour when he is in charge, and this is the reason why the head teacher sends him along. He is a good disciplinarian.

Briggs has always been happy with the *status quo*, where the brighter children work hard, pass examinations and go on to college or good jobs, while the less able get through school, struggle to gain any examination passes and end up in a factory. His attitudes have not changed with economic and social circumstances, which have ended the need for a vast pool of unskilled labour and destroyed employment opportunities for the pupils who will not pass examinations. In some ways he is less of a realist than Mrs Kay.

At the zoo, Briggs begins to thaw in his attitudes, appreciating the genuine if misdirected interest of the pupils in the animals, and starts to plan with Mrs Kay some interesting lessons using his slides. However, their 'borrowing' of the small animals and the reaction of the zoo keeper bring about a complete reversal: he yells at the children and regrets beginning to trust them. Unlike Mrs Kay, who can always forgive and start again, Briggs lacks the tolerance of mistakes to do so. After the scene with Carol on the cliff top, there is a deeper-seated change in Briggs. He really seems to have stood in Carol's shoes for a moment and seen the world from her perspective, and afterwards he insists on the visit to the fair, allowing the children to treat him as they do Mrs Kay and relaxing in their company. But the change is short lived. As the coach nears Liverpool and Mrs Kay takes her last photograph, reality returns, and the scene in which Mr Briggs deliberately exposes the film which is a record of his changed relationship with the Progress Class is one of the most poignant in the entire play.

By today's standards, Mr Briggs would possibly be judged as a good teacher because:
- He has consistently high expectations of pupils.
- His discipline is good and he sets high standards for behaviour.
- He plans learning experiences carefully and does not allow things to go wrong.

On the other hand:
- His attitudes are rigid.
- He is out of touch with his pupils and their lives.
- He is arrogant in his treatment of the children, and appears to care little for them.

COLIN & SUSAN

It is easier in many ways to treat these two **characters** together as their roles in the play are often parallel. Colin and Susan are two young teachers, either newly qualified or in their early years in teaching, and are full of enthusiasm and idealism. Like many young, spirited and dedicated teachers, they think that they can change the world. They represent optimism in the play and seem to offer some hope to the pupils in the Progress

Young and enthusiastic

Sympathetic and naïve

Friendly and sensible

Class; like Mrs Kay they are very much on the side of the children and wish to relate to them as people and improve their self-esteem and life chances. In some ways they are naïve; for example, they sometimes fail to maintain a professional distance, and probably reveal too much of their personal lives to the children. Susan's method of dealing with Brian Reilly's crush on her, while very effective and showing a good deal of common sense and knowledge of the psychology of teenage boys, could easily have backfired. In other ways, however, they are sensible and realistic, both in the way in which they relate to the children and in their handling of potential discipline problems or conflicts. In the scene where the bus makes a toilet stop, Colin realises that he lacks the authority born of experience which Briggs has, and which would enable him to make Brian put out his cigarette, but he wisely diffuses any confrontation in the technique he uses for persuading Brian to put it out.

The youth of Colin and Susan gives them, in one sense, much in common with the pupils in terms of understanding; they are only a few years older and can obviously relate to teenagers, having recently been there themselves. On the other hand, in terms of education, culture and opportunities, their lives are light years away from those of the Progress Class. They are educated, well-qualified professional people with reasonably good salaries and job security, as well as the attitudes developed through a university or college education. Their developing personal relationship underlines to Brian and Linda, the two teenagers who are particularly fond of Susan and Colin respectively, how bleak their own prospects are in comparison. The comments of the other children and the clear embarrassment of the two young teachers only serve to underline this for the audience. The subplot of Colin and Susan, Linda and Brian provides much of the **comedy** (see Literary Terms) in the play, but also serves to make the author's point about the waste of youthful energy and zest for life which the future in prospect for Brian and Linda shows. Even though there is a happy ending to this subplot, in that Linda ends up with Brian, leaving Colin and Susan to pursue their friendship in peace, the comments on the coach returning to Liverpool, where Brian remarks to Linda that he expects he will do 'nothing' when leaving school shortly, reminds the audience of the theme of waste and deprivation.

It is interesting to note that throughout the play Colin and Susan remain firmly on the side of Mrs Kay and the pupils, suggesting perhaps where the author's sympathies lie. Once, towards the **climax** (see Literary Terms) of Act II when Carol goes missing and Briggs turns on the other teachers with accusations of carelessness, Colin stands up to him, only to be crushed by Briggs's threats to finish him, Susan and Mrs Kay professionally on their return to school. Briggs may win the exchange, but the audience is clearly invited to sympathise with the other three teachers.

CAROL CHANDLER

Carol is an important **character** in the play in that she **symbolises** (see Literary Terms) the most deprived of children, and we are invited to share her perceptions of the world at several points in the action.

Carol's point of view is shown at the beginning of the play where she converses with Les: we see her excitement at the thought of going on a trip away from school and her complete lack of understanding of geography! We see the deprived inner-city environment through her eyes when she talks to Mrs Kay about it,

A victim
Warm hearted
and pathetic
Affectionate and
deprived
Inarticulate

and also the extent to which she is vaguely aware through what she has seen on television of a different, more pleasant world, when she comments on her wish for a house with a garden and trees outside.

She is among the least able of the pupils, being unable to master basic literacy skills which are the key to all learning, and therefore has a bleak educational future with no prospect of any examination passes. She also lacks confidence, self-esteem or social skills, relying heavily on adult guidance, and seems unable to remember simple information. Her lack of confidence is displayed at every turn: when she clings to Mrs Kay at the start of the trip demanding to know, like a much younger child, where they are going; when she asks her question, in one of the more poignant moments in the play, about learning to read and write so that she can live in a house with a garden; and when she pesters Mrs Kay about going home because she is so overwhelmed by the experience of the day out that she simply cannot face the end of it. She has spent so little time away from her inner-city, deprived environment that she thinks the sea is a lake and imagines that the coach will have to use a ferry to cross to Wales, only an hour's journey away by road. She clings to the security of Mrs Kay's company on the castle battlements, being perhaps unable to cope with the immensity of the castle and the sea. When the group are taken down to the beach she becomes obsessed with staying in Conway, recognising in some inarticulate way the poverty of her life as it is and not knowing how to express her anguish, apart from refusing to go home.

What Carol wants from life is extremely simple: she has no grandiose ideas about career success or becoming famous as one might expect from a young teenager, but wishes to live an ordinary life in a 'nice house' with a garden. What she desires as beyond her reach would be taken entirely for granted in the lives of many people, including her teachers, probably. Above all, she thinks she is in 'the fields of heaven' when brought on quite an ordinary day trip to Conway Castle, and she therefore has a special place in Mrs Kay's heart. Carol's outlook on life is bleak: she maintains that no-one will ever give anything to people like her because they do not take care of or deserve it, but she is astute enough to be aware, despite her low academic ability, of a few things, which she reveals in the scene on the cliff top with Briggs.

Consider why Carol is special.

Carol is driven onto the cliffs out of despair, and she tells Briggs in a moment of insight that he despises the pupils who come from backgrounds like hers, and only wants her down from the cliff edge because his career would be in trouble if she jumped over, not because he actually cares about her. She also recognises that if he had been her father, her life and opportunities would have been very different. In many ways she is a victim in the play, but she also has a warm heart and the author's sympathy is firmly with her.

LINDA CROXLEY

Linda is less of a victim than Carol, being well able to stand up for herself as she reveals in her first verbal exchange with Briggs in Act I. She is rude, insolent and dismissive of him, and he fails to get the better of her.

Linda is insolent, spirited and affectionate and has a certain wit and intelligence.

Throughout the play she reveals that she is a little more intelligent than some of the other pupils, not academically, but she has a certain native wit and a ready tongue.

The feeling Linda has for Colin is on one level a typical teenage 'crush' where a young girl loves someone unattainable before she is properly ready to fall in love with a suitable equal, but on another level serves to illustrate again the hopelessness of Linda's situation: she will never be able to call a man like Colin her equal. She will end up, because of the deprivation in her life and her low academic ability, repeating her mother's life, marrying a man who will be abusive or neglectful, and will leave her a single parent dependent on the state.

Linda is lively, enthusiastic and affectionate, despite her insolent and defensive manner with figures of authority like Mr Briggs. She genuinely likes Brian Reilly and towards the end of the play warmly responds to his tentative advances. We feel the sense of waste in the glimpse we are given of her future.

BRIAN REILLY

Cheeky

Disregards authority

Persistent

Puts on an act, but secretly unsure of himself

Good-humoured

Brian, like Linda, is cheeky and well able to stand up for himself with his peers or against authority when he wants to. He is no respecter of school rules, as he is rude to adults and slips off for a smoke whenever he can get away with it. He is only on the trip because he and his friend Digga are cheeky enough to ask Mrs Kay, knowing that she will be on their side and allow it. He has eventually learned to read and write and rejoined normal classes, but we sense that he will not achieve very good results, so his chance of a job seems as remote as that of any other child in the play. He is soon to leave school and expects to do nothing. Like many of the children, he comes from a home where his father has long ago left and there is little sense of him or any of the children having a happy family life.

Brian's cheeky and forward attitude extends to his blatant pursuit of Susan; he is not at all worried about making either her or Colin uncomfortable. Like many teenage boys who are perhaps more unsure of themselves than they would like to admit, he shows off

Consider the differences between Brian and Linda in the way they react to their teachers.

with a great deal of noise and bravado, pretending to be the world's greatest lover and openly telling Susan she would be better off with him than Colin because he is better looking and sexier. Of course, he knows that he has nothing to offer an educated woman like Susan and this makes him all the more jealous of Colin, as Linda is of Susan. But where Linda resents Susan silently, Reilly openly challenges Colin until the teacher admits to Susan that he is sick of the boy.

When Susan calls Reilly's bluff, he is quick to back away and reveals how unsure of himself he really is. He has liked Linda for some time, but been deceived by her harder insolent exterior and her feelings for Colin. She has not been as deceived; she admits to Colin that Brian is 'all right when you get him on his own'. Away from the male friends before whom he feels he has to keep up appearances, Brian has a gentler nature which, it is hinted, he has shown to Linda.

Although he lords it over smaller boys like the little kid and Andrews in the smoking scene on the coach, there is little malice in Brian; he teases Briggs good-humouredly at the end of the play about his transformation at the fair.

MINOR CHARACTERS

Ronnie

The bus driver begins by showing that he is prejudiced against the pupils from the more deprived schools, but is quickly talked by Mrs Kay into sympathising with them, and becomes a staunch supporter of the visit, suggesting extra stops to keep the children entertained, and joining in enthusiastically with them, even suggesting the game of football on the beach. He is generous, buying them sweets, and has a sense of fun, shown at the end when he asks if anyone has lost a small python; even the disaster at the zoo has amused him. Although the day out is just one of many school trips for which he drives the bus, we feel that he has really enjoyed this one and participated in a way he would not have done had the trip been from one of the ' better schools'.

Jackie

Linda's friend acts as her supporter throughout and to some extent shares her feelings for Colin, as she too pesters him on the coach and at the castle. She comments during Linda's song, 'I'm in Love with Sir', that Linda's future will mirror that of her own mother. So, of course, will Jackie's.

Digga

He is Brian's friend and acts in a similar way to Linda. Cheeky and defiant, he smokes on the coach and at the beach with Reilly, supports him in teasing Susan and Colin, and cheekily persuades Mrs Kay to take him on the trip in the first place. As the play concludes, with Brian and Linda together, he ends up with Jackie, perhaps a convenient reflection of their friendship.

Andrews

He is, like Carol, one of the most deprived children on the trip. He has jam sandwiches for lunch, provided by a mother who is a single parent trying desperately to survive against the background of his father disturbing them now and again when he wants money. He is a hopelessly addicted smoker, who seems to have a bleak future, but who comes up with some constructive suggestions for improving things during his conversation with Carol and Mrs Kay at the castle. Unlike Carol, he is an optimist who insists that if things were different and the children had something to call their own, they would respond by looking after it.

Milton

He is the barrack-room lawyer that every difficult school class appears to have. All his comments are played for **comedy** (see Literary Terms) as he points out obscure facts, like the number of people who die every year from ruptured bladders in order to lend weight to the argument about stopping for toilets. The audience laughs at his comments and the adults at whom they are directed probably feel like clipping him around the ear!

Two bored girls

Again a comic **chorus** (see Literary Terms) commenting on every stage of the trip. They are bored everywhere: on the coach, at the zoo, on the beach and at the fair. On leaving at the end of the day, they declare that it was wonderful. Every teacher has met a couple of children like these two, and they add to the **comedy**.

Other kids

These are again part of the **chorus**, joining in the songs and having occasional lines which contribute to the sense of fun and liveliness of the group, or serve to underline the deprivation of the pupils.

Head teacher

He represents the 'normal' school and really does not know how to deal with the Progress Class. He accepts Mrs Kay and her group as a necessary evil and a way of keeping these least able children out of the way of the rest of the school, but draws the line at allowing them to cause havoc out in the general community.

Les

He is used by the author to poke gentle fun at the hired labourer who will not deviate from the regulations because it is more than his 'job's worth'. There is also evidence of a friendly relationship with the more deprived children like Carol.

LANGUAGE & STYLE

Formal v. informal

There are a number of language forms used in *Our Day Out*.

There is first of all the contrast between the educated, formal tone of Mr Briggs and the more informal but still educated tone of Mrs Kay, Colin and Susan. Of

Consider the contrast between the teachers' language and that of the pupils.

the four teachers, Mrs Kay's language is least formal and therefore nearer to that of the children, but all four use **standard English** (see Literary Terms); Briggs virtually all the time and the other three most of the time. By contrast, the language of the children is that of Liverpool **dialect** (see Literary Terms), with uneducated speech forms predominant. In addition, the language of the song lyrics forms a contrast to that of the spoken parts of the play, with the songs often reflecting on the action, moving it forward, representing the passage of time, or bringing about a change in attitude.

Mr Briggs's language shows his inability to relax the role of teacher, and his distance from the world of the pupils. He displays a general inflexibility and lack of humour, and can sometimes sound pompous and confrontational.

Mrs Kay and the younger teachers speak fairly formally but with warmth and sympathy. They are not confrontational like Briggs but often sound persuasive and talk the pupils into behaving as they would wish. In the argument between Mrs Kay and Mr Briggs he continues to be pompous and inflexible while she is passionate and persuasive; the central theme of the play is laid before the audience in this scene and the strongly worded arguments of both characters invite the audience to make up their minds, although Mrs Kay is presented more sympathetically as usual.

Lack of education

The children's language reflects their lack of progress in education and the language they hear in the streets and at home. Endings are often left off words and there is a general sloppiness about speech. Slang and local **dialect** like 'goalie' and 'Shurrup' are often used. The violence of some of the language – 'You do an' I'll gob y" reflects the world of the youngsters. Much of the **dialogue** (see Literary Terms) in the play which involves the children is fast, snappy, lively and represents the quick streetwise wit typical of inner-city Liverpool.

The songs   The language of the songs often performs a different function, and as song lyrics the words involve repetition, or a **chorus** (see Literary Terms), which underlines the theme of each song. 'Look at the dogs' and 'Everywhere we go' represent the passing of time. Songs like 'I'm in love with Sir' and 'Why can't it always be this way' are sad and reflective, highlighting the plight of individual characters. The songs sung at the zoo, beach and fair are lively and full of repetition, describing the action and the fun at these places. 'Instructions on Enjoyment' and 'Castle Song' develop the **character** (see Literary Terms) of Mr Briggs and the others' response to him, while 'Straight Line ' **satirically** (see Literary Terms) underlines the differences in his attitudes and those of Mrs Kay. The songs generally add liveliness and warmth to the play, which otherwise might seem even more bleak.

Part four

Study skills

How to use quotations

One of the secrets of success in writing essays is the way you use quotations. There are five basic principles:

- Put inverted commas at the beginning and end of the quotation
- Write the quotation exactly as it appears in the original
- Do not use a quotation that repeats what you have just written
- Use the quotation so that it fits into your sentence
- Keep the quotation as short as possible

Quotations should be used to develop the line of thought in your essays.

Your comment should not duplicate what is in your quotation. For example:

Briggs tells Linda that he does not like her attitude: 'I don't like your attitude. I don't like it one bit.'

Far more effective is to write:

Briggs tells Linda: 'I don't like your attitude.'

The most sophisticated way of using the writer's words is to embed them into your sentence:

By the end of Act I Briggs feels that it is 'no wonder' that people won't do anything for the children as they act 'like animals'.

When you use quotations in this way, you are demonstrating the ability to use text as evidence to support your ideas - not simply including words from the original to prove you have read it.

Everyone writes differently. Work through the suggestions given here and adapt the advice to suit your own style and interests. This will improve your essay-writing skills and allow your personal voice to emerge.

The following points indicate in ascending order the skills of essay writing:

- Picking out one or two facts about the story and adding the odd detail
- Writing about the text by retelling the story
- Retelling the story and adding a quotation here and there
- Organising an answer which explains what is happening in the text and giving quotations to support what you write

....

- Writing in such a way as to show that you have thought about the intentions of the writer of the text and that you understand the techniques used
- Writing at some length, giving your viewpoint on the text and commenting by picking out details to support your views
- Looking at the text as a work of art, demonstrating clear critical judgement and explaining to the reader of your essay how the enjoyment of the text is assisted by literary devices, linguistic effects and psychological insights; showing how the text relates to the time when it was written

The dotted line above represents the division between lower- and higher-level grades. Higher-level performance begins when you start to consider your response as a reader of the text. The highest level is reached when you offer an enthusiastic personal response and show how this piece of literature is a product of its time.

*Coursework
essay*

Set aside an hour or so at the start of your work to plan what you have to do.

- List all the points you feel are needed to cover the task. Collect page references of information and quotations that will support what you have to say. A helpful tool is the highlighter pen: this saves painstaking copying and enables you to target precisely what you want to use.

- Focus on what you consider to be the main points of the essay. Try to sum up your argument in a single sentence, which could be the closing sentence of your essay. Depending on the essay title, it could be a statement about a character: Mrs Kay realises that the children have a bleak future and is therefore determined at least to give them a good day out; an opinion about language: Mr Briggs's formal language often shows how remote he is from the world of children like Reilly and Andrews when he lectures them on the architecture of the docks or on the evils of smoking, ignoring the problems in their families that they have just admitted to; or a judgement on a theme: One of the main themes is how coming from a deprived background can limit children's chances in life whatever they try to do to fight those limitations. Carol has no hope of a house with a garden while Reilly has no hope of a job when he leaves school, even though he has made enormous efforts to leave the Progress Class by learning to read and write.

- Make a short essay plan. Use the first paragraph to introduce the argument you wish to make. In the following paragraphs develop this argument with details, examples and other possible points of view. Sum up your argument in the last paragraph. Check you have answered the question.

- Write the essay, remembering all the time the central point you are making.

- On completion, go back over what you have written to eliminate careless errors and improve expression. Read it aloud to yourself, or, if you are feeling more confident, to a relative or friend.

If you can, try to type your essay using a word processor. This will allow you to correct and improve your writing without spoiling its appearance.

Examination essay

The essay written in an examination often carries more marks than the coursework essay even though it is written under considerable time pressure.

In the revision period build up notes on various aspects of the text you are using. Fortunately, in acquiring this set of York Notes on *Our Day Out*, you have made a prudent beginning! York Notes are set out to give you vital information and help you to construct your personal overview of the text.

Make notes with appropriate quotations about the key issues of the set text. Go into the examination knowing your text and having a clear set of opinions about it.

In most English Literature examinations you can take in copies of your set books. This is an enormous advantage although it may lull you into a false sense of security. Beware! There is simply not enough time in an examination to read the book from scratch.

In the examination

- Read the question paper carefully and remind yourself what you have to do.
- Look at the questions on your set texts to select the one that most interests you and mentally work out the points you wish to stress.
- Remind yourself of the time available and how you are going to use it.
- Briefly map out a short plan in note form that will keep your writing on track and illustrate the key argument you want to make.

- Then set about writing it.
- When you have finished, check through to eliminate errors.

To summarise,
these are keys
to success

- **Know the text**
- **Have a clear understanding of and opinions on the storyline, characters, setting, themes and writer's concerns**
- **Select the right material**
- **Plan and write a clear response, continually bearing the question in mind**

SAMPLE ESSAY PLAN

A typical essay question on *Our Day Out* is followed by a plan in note form. Try to add in your own ideas too.

Explore the differences in Mr Briggs's and Mrs Kay's views of education in *Our Day Out*. Write about how the author presents their views and how far you feel he sympathises with each.

Introduction

Mr Briggs and Mrs Kay present directly opposing views of education.

Views presented through words spoken, songs and reactions to pupils on the day trip.

Author's sympathy seems more with Mrs Kay though Briggs is given a substantial hearing.

Part 1

Briggs authoritarian; discipline and control important; give several examples of this.

Sent along by head; has position of power; give examples of where he reminds Mrs Kay of this.

Feels that the day out must be educational and not for fun; give examples of this view.

Part 2

Mrs Kay friendly and less formal; persuades children to behave sensibly rather than demanding absolute obedience; give examples of this.

Less powerful than Briggs; not even part of the mainstream school but tolerated by head because she keeps the least able 'out of the way'.

Feels that the children should enjoy the day and is not concerned about educational objectives; give examples from what she says.

Part 3   Briggs represents a traditional view: no tolerance of failure.

Abilities and social deprivation of children not taken into consideration.

Insists on high standards in uniform etc. and uses formal language.

Does not patronise, even though he shows little understanding of children as people.

Part 4   Mrs Kay makes allowances for deprivation of children and low ability.

She expects less from them because of their circumstances.

This could be construed as being patronising: the only way out of deprivation is by getting an education in order to get a job and break the cycle.

However, she considers the children's personal needs; give examples.

Part 5   Dramatic climax of the play: the argument between the teachers in Act II; these views passionately supported.

Language of Mrs Kay more sympathetic; does author support her?

Theme developed: social and economic changes have rendered these children redundant to society; at least she treats them as human beings not cogs in a machine. She actually wins the exchange and they stay at the beach.

Part 6   Next climax is scene with Carol. This appears to change Briggs's perceptions and he takes the group to the fair, showing a changed character.

However, the change only lasts as long as the trip, and he wilfully exposes the film which showed photographs of it.

The ending seems despairing as Carol and the others see him expose the film. Who is right: Briggs or Mrs Kay?

The final song supports Mrs Kay, showing that she has succeeded in giving the kids something special that no-one can take away.

Conclusion   Some ambivalence, as both arguments are strongly presented.

Briggs fails to change, but nor does Mrs Kay alter her attitude.

Ending supports her views.

Personal view in conclusion.

FURTHER QUESTIONS

Here are some more questions. Work out what your answer would be, always being sure to draw up a plan first.

1 Who would you prefer as a teacher, Mrs Kay or Mr Briggs? Who would give you the better education? Support what you say by close reference to the play.

2 Consider the role of Carol in the play. Does she have your sympathy, and in what ways does the author use her to present some of the themes?

3 The play is about waste, the waste of human lives. Show how the author makes this clear, and how he saves the audience from despair.

4 *Our Day Out* has been heavily criticised for showing the worst side of young people: anti-authoritarian attitudes, bad language, vandalism and theft. How would you defend it against this criticism?

5 How does the author make us laugh at the mischief of the children, and cry at the bleakness of their futures, in one very short play? You should consider:
- the language
- the role of the songs
- the characters and action

6 Why should pupils study this play for examinations or coursework? What can they learn from it?

7 Choose three incidents in the play which you consider to be comic. Show how the author has created good comedy out of the characters, events and dialogue in your chosen scenes.

8 Choose two characters with whom you sympathise, and two whom you find less sympathetic, in *Our Day Out*. Write about each character, bringing out the ways in which the author makes you feel sympathy or lack of it.

10 A lot of the events in *Our Day Out* are funny because they are typical of school trips. Choose three events or scenes from the play which you think are typical and explain how the author has used language, dialogue and the characters to make them amusing for the audience.

11 A critic once said that it was obvious that Willy Russell had never been a teacher because no teacher in their right mind would ever run such a disastrous day trip. How realistic do you find the play? In your answer you should consider:
- The characters and the way they interact
- The events of the day
- The language and dialogue of the play

PART FIVE

CULTURAL CONNECTIONS

BROADER PERSPECTIVES

It would probably be helpful to view the BBC television version of *Our Day Out* (1976) if it is available. Made as a straight play without the songs, which were added later (see Introduction) it should prove an enjoyable alternative version of the drama.

To understand Willy Russell as a contemporary playwright, it would be useful to read or see a performance of one of his other plays which deals with the theme of education or of wasted opportunities for the young from deprived areas.

Educating Rita is often set as an A level text and has also been filmed (see Introduction). The play was written for only two characters: Doctor Bryant, the university lecturer, and Rita, the mature Open University student whose tutor he becomes. Rita is a 'second chance' student, a hairdresser in her mid-twenties who left school in her teens without qualifications but has always felt that she can learn. As her education transforms her during the course of the play, she can no longer inhabit the working-class inner-city world from which she began and has to decide where her priorities lie. The film version introduces all the other characters who are mentioned in the original script. Like *Our Day Out*, the play deals thoughtfully on several levels with the purpose and function of education, and the effects of social background and class culture on educational and life chances. It is less bleak than *Our day Out* but contains the same mixture of the comic and the sense of tragic waste of life that lack of education can mean for individuals.

Another play by Willy Russell which deals with opportunity in a less specifically educational sense is

Stags and Hens, a comedy (see Literary Terms) which takes place in a night club where a young couple about to get married are out on their respective stag and hen nights, unaware of each other's presence in the club. Many of the same themes of opportunity, or lack of it, as they are affected by culture and social class, are explored. The play was dramatised for television under the title *Dancin' Thru' the Dark*.

Other books which deal with the effect of deprivation on educational and life chances include *A Kestrel for a Knave* by Barry Hines (Penguin, 1968) which deals with fifteen-year-old Billy, from an inner-city housing estate, and the ways in which his family, social environment and education limit his chances. His only escape from a downward spiral into petty crime seems to be in his relationship with his kestrel hawk, Kes. The novel has also been filmed by Ken Loach.

Buddy by Nigel Hinton (Heinemann, 1982) is a novel which deals with adolescence and the problems of growing up and succeeding educationally with an absent parent. Following Buddy's father's involvement in petty crime and their difficult home circumstances, his mother leaves, and like many of the characters in *Our Day Out*, he has to learn to manage without her.

atmosphere a common term for the mood – moral, sensational, emotional, or intellectual – which dominates a piece of writing

character characters are the invented, imaginary persons in a dramatic work which are given human qualities and behaviour

chorus in the tragedies of the ancient Greek playwrights, the chorus is a group of characters who represent ordinary people in their attitudes to the action which they witness and on which they comment. The children, rather than specific characters, in *Our Day Out* often act as a chorus when they use the songs to comment on environment or action

climax any point of great intensity in a literary work; the culminating moment of the action. There are two climactic scenes in *Our Day Out*: one where Briggs and Mrs Kay argue passionately on the castle ramparts about the purpose of the day out and the future of the children, and one where Briggs discovers Carol on the cliff edge and she threatens to jump off

colloquialism the use of the kinds of expression and grammar associated with ordinary everyday speech rather than formal language. The speech of the children is regarded as colloquial

comedy a broad genre which encompasses many different kinds of literature, but is most often used for drama which is designed to entertain and ends happily. *Our Day Out* is comedy tinged with pathos and realism, which does not have the conventional happy ending for all the characters

dialect the speech peculiar to a particular area or locality, with specialist vocabulary typical of speech rather than writing. In *Our Day Out* the dialect used is that of Liverpool

dialogue the speech and conversation between characters in any kind of literary work

diatribe an angry or uncontrolled verbal attack on someone or something. Mr Briggs's attack on Mrs Kay could be said to be a diatribe

episodic drama or narrative written in the form of a series of separable incidents

farce comedy which borders on the absurd

idiom a way of expressing things special to a particular language or dialect

interlude a short dramatic scene within a drama

irony consists of saying one thing while you mean another, or of showing one thing in a drama while pointing to a completely opposite meaning: e.g., the name 'Progress Class' for those children who have made the least progress!

musical a play whose action is partly depicted in songs, which may indicate the passing of time, describe events or add insight into a character

pathos moments in works of art which evoke strong feelings of pity and sorrow are said to have this quality

realism telling things as they are, often in haphazard detail, evoking real experiences. Rather vague as a term, but much of the dialogue in *Our Day Out* which evokes the lives of the children could be said to be realistic

reprise a repeat of a song performed earlier

satire literature which examines vice and folly and makes them appear ridiculous

standard English the language of formal discourse or writing, rather than that of everyday conversation

stereotype an ordinary common place perception made dull by constant repetition

structure the overall principle of organisation in a work of literature

style the characteristic manner in which a writer expresses him or herself, or the particular manner of an individual literary work

stylised overtly and exaggeratedly in the style of drama; rather than realistically presented

symbol a material object, or sometimes a character in a play, used by the author to represent something invisible like an idea or quality

tableau a pictorial grouping of persons in a drama

TEST ANSWERS

TEST YOURSELF (Section 1)

A
1 Ronnie
2 Brian Reilly
3 Carol
4 Mrs Kay
5 Linda
6 Mr Briggs

TEST YOURSELF (Section 2)

A
1 Milton
2 Mr Briggs
3 Mr Briggs
4 Linda
5 Mrs Kay

TEST YOURSELF (Section 3)

A
1 Mr Briggs
2 Carol
3 Mrs Kay
4 Mr Briggs
5 Brian Reilly

TEST YOURSELF (Section 4)

A
1 Mrs Kay
2 Brian Reilly
3 Ronnie
4 Carol
5 Mr Briggs
6 Mr Briggs

TITLES IN THE YORK NOTES SERIES

GCSE and equivalent levels (£3.50 each)

Maya Angelou
I Know Why the Caged Bird Sings

Jane Austen
Pride and Prejudice

Harold Brighouse
Hobson's Choice

Charlotte Brontë
Jane Eyre

Emily Brontë
Wuthering Heights

Charles Dickens
David Copperfield

Charles Dickens
Great Expectations

Charles Dickens
Hard Times

George Eliot
Silas Marner

William Golding
Lord of the Flies

Willis Hall
The Long and the Short and the Tall

Thomas Hardy
Far from the Madding Crowd

Thomas Hardy
The Mayor of Casterbridge

Thomas Hardy
Tess of the d'Urbervilles

L.P. Hartley
The Go-Between

Seamus Heaney
Selected Poems

Susan Hill
I'm the King of the Castle

Barry Hines
A Kestrel for a Knave

Louise Lawrence
Children of the Dust

Harper Lee
To Kill a Mockingbird

Laurie Lee
Cider with Rosie

Arthur Miller
A View from the Bridge

Arthur Miller
The Crucible

Robert O'Brien
Z for Zachariah

George Orwell
Animal Farm

J.B. Priestley
An Inspector Calls

Willy Russell
Educating Rita

Willy Russell
Our Day Out

J.D. Salinger
The Catcher in the Rye

William Shakespeare
Henry V

William Shakespeare
Julius Caesar

William Shakespeare
Macbeth

William Shakespeare
A Midsummer Night's Dream

William Shakespeare
The Merchant of Venice

William Shakespeare
Romeo and Juliet

William Shakespeare
The Tempest

William Shakespeare
Twelfth Night

George Bernard Shaw
Pygmalion

R.C. Sherriff
Journey's End

Rukshana Smith
Salt on the snow

John Steinbeck
Of Mice and Men

R.L. Stevenson
Dr Jekyll and Mr Hyde

Robert Swindells
Daz 4 Zoe

Mildred D. Taylor
Roll of Thunder, Hear My Cry

Mark Twain
The Adventures of Huckleberry Finn

James Watson
Talking in Whispers

A Choice of Poets

Nineteenth Century Short Stories

Poetry of the First World War

Six Women Poets

Advanced level (£3.99 each)

Margaret Atwood
The Handmaid's Tale

William Blake
Songs of Innocence and of Experience

Emily Brontë
Wuthering Heights

Geoffrey Chaucer
The Wife of Bath's Prologue and Tale

Joseph Conrad
Heart of Darkness

Charles Dickens
Great Expectations

F. Scott Fitzgerald
The Great Gatsby

Thomas Hardy
Tess of the d'Urbervilles

James Joyce
Dubliners

Arthur Miller
Death of a Salesman

William Shakespeare
Antony and Cleopatra

William Shakespeare
Hamlet

William Shakespeare
King Lear

William Shakespeare
The Merchant of Venice

William Shakespeare
Romeo and Juliet

William Shakespeare
The Tempest

Mary Shelley
Frankenstein

Alice Walker
The Color Purple

Tennessee Williams
A Streetcar Named Desire